ADVANCE PRAISE

"*The Accidental Suffragist* is the so-timely story of the sacrifices one mother makes—to her family, her safety, and her previous identity—when called by a cause and stirred to act. Through the telling of this factory worker's experience, Gichon reminds us of the grave sacrifices so many women made more than a century ago and the debt of gratitude we owe them today as we see Kamala Harris's ascent to Vice President. My teenage daughters snatched this book from my hands before I could even finish." **Alisyn Camerota**, CNN Anchor and Author of *Amanda Wakes Up*

"*The Accidental Suffragist* is a poignant and memorable story sweeping the reader through an early 20th century labor tragedy to the ache of a son going off to war. All told through the eyes of a wife and mother who wants no more than to do all she can for her family. When the suffrage movement pulls her into the cause, she at last realizes that voting will be her only hope of having her voice heard. Written with heart and relatability, the modern day reader will not be able to help feeling a profound sense of gratitude for all that was endured by our sisters before us." **Camille Di Maio**, Bestselling author of *The First Emma*

"*The Accidental Suffragist* is a compelling exploration of the early twentieth century movement to provide women the right to vote, with an endearing protagonist and plenty of fascinating historical detail." **Kimmery Martin**, Author of *The Antidote for Everything*

"With its captivating heroine and rich historical details, *The Accidental Suffragist* is a novel that both enlightens and enthralls. A must-read for those interested (and we all should be!) in the fight waged by brave American women determined to secure their right to vote." **Nina Sankovitch**, Author and Historian

"Through the eyes of an unlikely activist, novelist Galia Gichon masterfully takes readers inside the inner circle of the brave women fighting for the right to vote at the turn of the 20th Century. Inspirational and enlightening, this work of historical fiction pulls the reader in from the first page. A perfect read for mothers and daughters to discuss and enjoy together." **Heather Cabot**, Author of *The New Chardonnay*

"*The Accidental Suffragist* is an entertaining, meticulously researched novel about the struggles and eventual triumphs of the suffragist cause in the early twentieth century. Within this fascinating historical context, Gichon also explores the challenge and compromise inherent to working motherhood, a topic equally relevant today as it was then." **Heather Frimmer**, Author of *Better to Trust* and *Bedside Manners*

"Many women wish the world was a kinder, fairer place for them, some women make it so. Gichon, like her heroines, moves through the world fueled by love and a sense of justice, the result is a richly detailed and studiously researched novel that will bring hope to your heart." **Lorea Canales**, Author of *Becoming Marta*

"Gichon's *The Accidental Suffragist* is a multidimensional, fascinating and unputdownable story—and important for this moment. She takes the readers on a journey brimming with captivating feminist history. This debut fiction novel couldn't be more timely." **Lindsey Pollak**, author of *Recalculating: Navigate Your Career Through the Changing World of Work*

"More so than most fictionalized accounts, *The Accidental Suffragist* holds a compelling and intriguing approach that readers will find enlightening and involving. It's highly recommended even for those well aware of the changing politics of the times, early women's rights movements, and the factory fire's lasting impact." **Midwest Book Review**

The Accidental Suffragist

The Accidental Suffragist

~ *a novel* ~

GALIA GICHON

Wyatt-MacKenzie Publishing
DEADWOOD, OREGON

The Accidental Suffragist

Galia Gichon

ISBN: 978-1-948018-96-8

Library of Congress Control Number: 2021936450

Wyatt-MacKenzie Publishing
DEADWOOD, OREGON

Wyatt-MacKenzie Publishing, Inc.
Deadwood, Oregon

www.WyattMacKenzie.com

For Sophie and Hannah

PART 1

CHAPTER 1

January 1911. New York City. Lower East Side

HELEN FOX WALKED UP to her building, dodging wayward neighborhood boys chasing a stray dog, grabbing the last few moments of daylight. Before stepping over the onion peels and picked-over chicken carcasses on the sidewalk, she wrinkled her nose as a carted horse dropped manure in front of the building; she then hastened her way up the stairs. Pausing in the foyer, she raised her arms over her head to stretch her back from being hunched over a sewing machine all day at her job at McKee Button Factory. The closing bell still clanged in her ears. Nearly thirty years old, she wore a high-necked shirt tucked into a simple brown cotton skirt. She sighed as she saw the dust coating her clothing.

As she eased down the tight dark hallway, she almost didn't stop at the mailboxes, giving them just her usual cursory glance. Then a bright white envelope in the slot marked with their apartment number caught her eye. Surprised, she reached for it, examined "Fox Family" written in swooping calligraphy. The return address was unfamiliar. She stood for a long moment just looking at the envelope. Feeling the weight of the paper in her hands, she started to get excited—something she didn't feel very often. Something good was in this envelope. She looked over at the other mailboxes. Had her neighbors received one as well? No, but there was another envelope in her box. Two pieces of mail! This one was a bill and Helen's heart sank. She knew that the doctor's visit for Eleanor a few weeks ago would come back to haunt her. Putting both envelopes in her skirt pocket, she'd deal with them later. She could savor the heavy envelope later when the children were asleep. Her four children—Abigail, 12, Walter, 10, Claudia, 8 and Eleanor, 4—were waiting upstairs for her to start supper before her husband, Albert, came home. After climbing the stairs, she hesitated at the front door, stood straight, and tucked in the long brunette hairs that had fallen loose. Worry lines prematurely settled in her forehead and around her mouth.

"Hello Mama," Abigail, her eldest, said and kissed Helen on the cheek as she entered the main area of their two-room apartment. The sofa sat in the center, doubling as Helen and Albert's bed at night, with a small kitchen set against the wall by the window facing the street. Shelves holding plates and teacups hung above the limited counter. The only other furniture in the main room was a square wooden table with four mismatched chairs. The one bedroom, separated by a faded cream curtain with small flowers, had a bed where the children slept and a pine four-drawer dresser that held all the family's clothing.

"How was your day?" Abigail asked.

Helen thought about the foreman at her factory, at the end of the day, who stood by the door, holding it open with his dirty gray boot, dangling a set of keys from his fingertips, grinning, and saying, "See you in the morning, ladies." They'd been locked in the factory all day.

"Good, good, had a nice chat with Iris on the way home," she said, squaring her shoulders, stroking the back of her neck, then walking over to a basin in the kitchen where she cleaned her hands to get the dirt out from under her fingernails. They didn't need to know.

Abigail went back to the counter and resumed chopping celery for the supper stew.

"Ouch!" she cried out.

"What?" Helen rushed over. She grabbed Abigail's arm and saw the blood.

"It's ok. Just a nick," Abigail reassured, covering the wound with the cloth from the counter.

"You must be more careful. That girl last week at the factory, you remember I told you? The one who cut off her finger. She still isn't back to work. I heard she has an infection." Helen fingered the doctor bill in her skirt pocket.

"Yes, Mama."

Helen composed herself and focused on Claudia and Eleanor; her eyes gleamed and mouth curved into a smile as she saw Claudia chopping potatoes for the stew and Eleanor, in the middle of the kitchen covered in black dust. She was pitching in, gathering coal from the storage area to heat their rooms. Helen walked over to her and patted her dress creating a black swirl.

"Let's get you cleaned up little one." Then she scooped her up in her arms, not caring that the dust was getting all over her as well.

Noises came from the street and Abigail stood by the grimy window, observing children standing on a stranded horse cart watching a game of stickball while drying laundry flapped over them on a clothesline between two buildings. They tightly clutched baskets filled with items foraged from the streets. None of them looked as if they had bathed in weeks; dirt smudged on foreheads, shirts untucked, uncombed hair.

Albert burst into the apartment, "I got a few more guys to come to our next meeting. It's a great start." The children all crowded around him by the front door, eager to hear his update.

"Papa, Joe at school said you spoke to his father," Walter said.

"Did he say he was going?"

"Don't know. He said he didn't want any trouble. Are you in trouble?"

"Nah. Not at all."

"Please tell me the owners don't know yet what you're doing. If you lose your job ... the can in the closet has even fewer coins," Helen stated. For weeks now, Albert had been coming home late from attending union meetings at his factory job and was now furtively organizing a group.

"Stop your worrying, Helen. We'll be fine. Change is coming and we can't stop it!" he bellowed, taking off his boots, durable workwear coat, and flat cap. He had hazel eyes from his English ancestors, a full head of chestnut hair that he slicked back with pomade every morning and still stood lean and tall even though he spent countless hours hunched daily over heavy machines in the garment factory.

~

Later that evening, after the children were asleep, Helen undressed, getting ready for bed. She found the thick envelope in her skirt pocket. She took it out, opened it; her eyes widened and lips parted slightly.

"What's that?" Albert asked.

"An Invitation to Afternoon Tea. From Mrs. Theodore Fraser," she read out loud.

"Mrs. Fraser? Who's that?"

"Rosie Smith. Remember married to the rich fellow?" Helen said trying to be nonchalant. "Rosie was ice-skating in Central Park and met Ted Fraser. Turned out he was awfully rich, living right on Gramercy Park. In no time, they got married." She left out how Rosie's beautiful face and easy laughter helped Ted overlook her modest background. Plus, the scandalous details of the baby boy born seven months after the wedding. The whole neighborhood was shocked and envious, including Helen, who'd always been friendly with her.

"Tea? You've never been to tea," he said.

"Well, there's always a first time."

"You can't go."

"But Albert, we have to!"

"I won't allow it." She did need his permission to attend this event; she just didn't ask to go out alone very often.

"Albert ...."

"It's not our place."

"But it'll be good for us; for the girls, for me. We need some happiness, Albert. We don't get many—any invitations in fact."

"No, Helen. We just don't mix with those kind of folks, especially now that I'm fighting the fat-cat owners of the factories."

"Albert, you're making changes—why can't we?"

"My changes are different, for a better life for us. You know that. This invitation ..." he pointed and shrugged it away, "does not."

"Can't we just give our girls a glimpse of a better life?"

"They're never going to get the better life that way. I said 'NO' Helen. End of discussion." They got into their sofa bed, pulled at the quilt to warm up, trying to put aside the tension thick between them. Abigail came out quietly from the bedroom and crawled into the tight space between them.

"Mama, Papa. I can help," she said softly.

"Help with what?" Helen asked.

"A better life. I can go work, in the factory with you."

"Abigail, you're not going to work in a factory or anywhere else!" She glared at Albert. "We have plenty." Though they both knew there wasn't enough and Abigail would end up going to work. They had arrived at the same decision when Helen went to work in the factory. There just wasn't enough money from Albert's paycheck at the time to feed and warm the family.

Even with Helen working, there wasn't enough now.

"Come dear, let me tuck you back to sleep. You need a good night's rest for school tomorrow," Helen said quickly and rose from the sofa bed. She escorted Abigail back to the warm bed she shared with her siblings, clutching her nightgown with a bunched-up fist. The invitation would have to wait for now.

"We do need the extra money, Helen, and she wants to help out," Albert said as they both settled down to try and sleep. Helen took a big sigh and tried to put the day behind her.

CHAPTER 2
March 1911

HELEN HUNCHED OVER the sewing machine at the button factory, her foot moving up and down to make the mechanics move along. She struggled to keep her eyes open from the monotony of sewing buttons all day and the whirring noise of the machines. The coal furnace powering the large ironing machines overheated the factory room and the droning of the machines with their lines of buttons waiting to be sewn combined to make her drowsy. Helen wiped beads of sweat from her forehead even though the temperature outside hovered around 30 degrees. It had been more than a month since Abigail had started her own job at a factory. They had lost the fight with her and ultimately needed the extra money. The conditions, from the little she shared, seemed to be the same. It was almost the end of her shift when she felt a hand on her shoulder, startling her from her work trance.

"Helen, the foreman wants you. In his office," a woman's voice said, pointing towards the foreboding dark corner of an office walled in with heavy paneled wooden doors.

What have I done? She thought and stood up, walking towards the office, only seeing hazy figures through the door. She knocked and heard a muffled response to come in.

"You asked to see me?" she asked tentatively walking into his office.

"You are ...?" he said without looking up from the sheet of paper in his hand.

"Mrs. Fox, Helen Fox."

He looked his sheet of paper up and down and then turned it over. The writing on the paper was very small and he took his glasses off to read it closer. Even though the factory was so warm, he wore a vest and jacket over his starched white shirt.

"There's been an accident at the Triangle Shirtwaist Factory," the foreman said. Before he even finished his sentence, Helen ran out of his office, without her coat and handbag, flew down the stairs and sprinted the multiple blocks from her factory to Abigail's factory.

"Please let Abigail be safe. Please let Abigail be safe," she mouthed over and over as she ran, her feet barely touching the ground. She prayed in her head, trying to recall psalms from childhood buried deep. Within a few blocks, she was panting so hard; she could only utter:

"Safe, Safe, Safe ...."

Helen smelled smoke before she saw anything. She rounded the corner to Abigail's factory. The smell got stronger as she turned onto the street where the building was, stinging her eyes, while wisps of gray smoke curled above her. She ran closer towards the building, the smoke getting progressively darker. Her thin cotton shirt was damp with perspiration and she was out of breath, but she kept running, not stopping for a moment to catch her breath.

She had prayed over and over that it was an error and the fire was at another factory but when she saw a crowd of people gathered in front of a building there was no mistaking this was where Abigail worked.

The crowd was a mixture of curious onlookers and concerned people looking for someone. For a moment, they seemed orderly and then it switched to people jostling and pushing each other to get to the front of the crowd, as close to the building as possible. Helen pushed her way, elbowing anyone in her way with fierce determination to get to the front, not saying a word. Two policemen stood there yelling at the crowd, "Get back! Let the lads do their work. You're just getting in their way."

"My baby's in there. I need to save her," Helen barked so fiercely, the people around her gave her some space.

"Get back. They're working their best to get them out," the policemen bellowed back over her head, their arms stretched out attempting to keep the crowd at bay. It almost didn't matter that the policemen were keeping the crowd back from rushing the building, they wouldn't have been able to get any further. Helen stood at the front and felt the heat from the fire slap her body, almost knocking her down. The heat felt like it was searing any exposed skin, warding off the cold air and heating her body. She then looked up and saw the actual fire.

She was so close to the front, she had to crane her neck, arching it as far back as it would go, so she could look up and see as much of the building as she could. It seemed that flames were shooting from all of the ten floors of the building.

"Watch your step," a policeman shouted, which brought Helen's attention back to the street. She saw a handful of men, their caps slung low on their heads, dragging bodies that were laid on the street to clear the path the firemen were using. They were listless and lifeless bodies of young girls, their arms and legs in awkward positions. Helen quickly scanned their faces, holding her breath, her mouth grimaced, looking for any familiar sign.

"Abigail? Abigail?"

None of them were her daughter. She let out a huge breath. Their bodies were soon out of the way so the firemen had a clear path to go back and forth doing their job of attempting to put out the fire.

Flames were now shooting out of every window. The firemen were throwing buckets of water from their horse and carriage trucks onto the building, trying to put out the blazing fire. Their hurried movements seemed futile against the out-of-control blazes. Helen whipped her head, looking around wildly. She felt sizzling sparks licking at her face. She looked around to see the firemen riskily place ladders against the heated building.

"There's no way those ladders will reach the girls' floors," the woman next to Helen remarked.

"They have to! Our girls are in there. What floor?" Helen answered, slightly embarrassed she didn't know what floor Abigail worked on.

"Tenth floor," the woman answered. Helen quickly counted the number of floors, pointing to each one. The ladders weren't tall enough.

The flames were very high, coming out of every window and open crevice; windows breaking from the heat, most of them broken by now. Helen stood there, hypnotized in disbelief. She stared at the windows, swearing she saw ominous eyes peeking from behind the windows, glaring and begging for help. Each snap of the fire and crack of a window felt like an individual shard of glass hitting her body with cutting and intense pain. The crackle of the fire kept getting louder and the heat more intense. It almost was too hot on her face, but she couldn't take even one step back to retreat in case she missed seeing Abigail. She felt the cold air pocket for a moment on her back, making her damp shirt feel icier, a sharp contrast to the searing heat on her face. She didn't want to allow herself to be warmed by the heat. She couldn't just stand there any longer.

"What's happening? Please help me! My daughter's in there, you have to get her out!" she pleaded to a fireman rushing by with a bucket of water in each hand. No answer. Another fireman right behind her, pushed her hard.

"Lady, get out of our way!"

"Has anyone come out?" she tried someone else: a policeman. He shook his head.

"My daughter's in there," she screamed at him.

"I know, Lady. We're doing the best we can. Let the lads put out the flames."

"Her name's Abigail. Scream and see if Abigail answers," she beseeched at two firemen running by with a ladder that finally looked longer and would maybe reach the higher floors. They didn't respond.

The crowd kept pushing up against her, elbows jostling her ribs, hands on her back as people moved around desperate for a sign. She kept turning around facing the fire then back to the crowd then facing the fire again. Not wanting to lose her front row position. She searched for a familiar face. Looking for Abigail. Maybe she escaped through a side door? Maybe she had left early? More people kept showing up, crowding the sidewalk. She feverishly looked for Abigail's face in the crowd but didn't find her. The faces started to blend together, everyone appearing the same, yet unfamiliar. She started hysterically crying, unable to hold in her sobs any longer. People around her, were asking, many in heavy accents:

"Have you seen ...."

"My daughter ...."

Names were being called out, swirling in the sky above: "Angela, Carmela, Sarah, Bessie, Rose, Donna, Anna, Maria, Rita ...."

The smoke got thicker, black at this point, making it hard to see the people; the crowd became denser as more onlookers arrived: other women who had left their sweatshop or domestic jobs, men from their factory work and children from the nearby tenements looking for a sibling or a family member. All watching the horror blaze before them. Another listless body lay on the sidewalk. She moved close to see the face. The girl looked about the same age as Abigail, same brunette hair, with a long braid to one side of her face, just like Abigail wore. She even had on a similar outfit: off white work shirt tucked into a dark blue wool skirt. It wasn't Abigail. But it was someone else's daughter.

Helen had to step back from the front of the crowd to get away from the heat of the fire and the smoke. Maybe Abigail was looking for her closer to the street. As she stepped onto the middle of the street, she felt a tap on her shoulder.

"Dear, dear, what's happened?" She turned around and saw an older woman, finely dressed with a group of similarly dressed women.

"My daughter, Abigail's in there," Helen answered, garbling her words between cries. She was desperate for contact, hoping someone had answers or could help her. A younger woman in the group said, "I just heard there are no survivors."

Helen's knees turned to jelly, she could no longer stand up and felt blood rush to her head. Everything turned black.

CHAPTER 3

Harriot's Parlor

HELEN OPENED HER EYES, slowly. The room was bright, yet the darkened windows confused her. She took a deep breath and smelled jasmine perfume. She put her arm over her eyes to block out the light and smelled smoke on her shirt. The room felt warm and stuffy. Where was she?

The fire.

No survivors.

Oh no. The memory hurled back to Helen and she tried to get up but her hips only shifted slightly. She realized she was on a couch. It was so soft. This wasn't her couch in the apartment. The fabric felt plush and smooth under her fingers. She tried to sit up again but felt dizzy and fell back down. She opened her eyes and saw dark blue velvet.

How did she get here? Where was she? A face appeared, "Abigail?" Helen asked. The woman simply shook her head. Then whispered, "There were no survivors."

Helen burst into sobs, heaving heavy silent cries, covering her eyes with her hands, not wanting this stranger to see her cry. What was she going to do? Her baby. Her baby. Abigail. The woman pulled up a chair, sat, and started stroking her head.

"Dear, take this," she handed her a thick wet warmed-up cloth, "put it on your face." Helen recognized her as the older woman from outside Abigail's factory. She lay her head back down with the washcloth on her face. It shut the world out for a spell. Perhaps when she opened her eyes, this nightmare would be over.

"Please sip this tea," Helen heard and shook her head.

"It'll be good for you, I'm sure you haven't drunk or eaten anything in hours."

She sat up and a different hand gave her a cup and saucer. She took a sip. The formal china made her nervous, her hands were shaking; she didn't want the teacup to break. It did taste delicious; she was thirsty and felt her stomach rumble. The older woman kept patting her shoulder and head; her silk dress rubbed against Helen's hand, which felt awkwardly reassuring even though it was coming from a complete stranger. Helen looked around, gazing at the elegant and opulent room, not wanting to make eye contact with this woman sitting next to her. There were thick Persian rugs on the floor, large oil paintings hanging on the walls over ornate bright wallpaper, crystal gas lamps in the corners and on carved wood side tables. They shined so bright. She'd never been in a room this elegant before. What was she doing here?

"I need to look for Abigail—she's waiting for me at home," Helen murmured but felt too dizzy to move. She shut her eyes for a moment. Then opened them and looked at the woman sitting next to her. Her face was lined, and she was smiling at her, warmth emanating from her face. She was slight, almost petite, yet she looked strong. Her deep purple silk dress tucked in at the waist and had a high collar and puffed shoulder sleeves. Helen couldn't see her shoes, as the woman's dress reached the ground, but she was sure they were polished and unscuffed.

"Is Abigail your daughter?"

"She is. She must be so worried I'm not home yet," she nodded with closed eyes. She heard voices from another room; they weren't alone. "Where am I?" she asked.

Why wasn't Albert at the factory? she suddenly thought about her husband, recalling other men there.

"You are in the sitting room in my home. We were speaking to you at the ... factory and you fainted. You were there alone and no one knew you—we asked around. My carriage was close by, hence Alice and the others helped get you into the carriage and into the house."

"Who are you?" she asked, not meaning to sound as rude as it did.

"Oh dear, how impolite I've been. Please let me introduce myself. I'm Harriot Stanton Blatch. Please tell us your name and we will get you home," she put her hand out to Helen to shake it. Helen limply shook back.

Helen cleared her throat. She coughed and then spoke in a low whisper, "I'm Helen Fox and my daughter Abigail works in the Triangle Shirtwaist Factory. I need to get home to my family." She tried to stand, but still felt lightheaded and sat back down.

"We'll get you home. Sit dear, you clearly aren't ready to go anywhere. You are in no state to walk home." Helen overhead women talking in the other room, catching snippets of their conversation.

"She barely looks old enough to have children."

"Apparently her daughter, Abigail, was working in the factory."

"We should get her home."

"This is an outrage, we have to do something. This never should have happened."

Two women walked in to the sitting room, their long skirts swishing slightly. Helen watched the smooth motion of the expensive linen fabric shift.

"Hello, I'm Alice Paul."

"I'm Lucy Burns." They did not offer their hands to shake.

"We are so ... sorry." The silence was awkward.

"Why were you at the fire?" Helen asked. All these women were more the type to wear the clothing, not sew them.

Alice spoke. "We heard about the fire. We are suffragists; we work with Harriot. We are also part of a labor group to stop hiring underage children. We had been trying to talk with the owners of The Triangle Shirtwaist Factory for some time but ... " Lucy grabbed Alice's wrist to signal that she should stop talking.

Shut up, shut up, you fool! One of those underage children is my daughter. My beautiful daughter. Her name is Abigail Fox. She's a beautiful twelve-year-old girl. Just a baby, Helen thought as big fat silent tears rolled down her cheek, putting her hands over her ears, her eyes clenched shut. She didn't want to cry anymore in front of these strangers. She had to get out of there. She looked around and the walls were closing in on her. She needed to escape and see her children, Albert. She needed to see Abigail.

She rose, "Please show me the way out."

"Helen, please let us arrange a carriage to take you home," said Harriot.

"No, I can walk."

"No, no, you are in no state, it's dark out."

"I've left my purse at my factory." The words "my factory" sounded dirty in this elegant room.

Even if she had her purse, there weren't any coins to take a carriage home, which these women were oblivious to. Helen brushed her shirt, now tinged gray from the smoke, in a futile attempt to brush off dirt and ashes. She tucked stray hairs back into her bun.

"Helen, I meant my carriage. My driver is outside. He's done feeding the horses and will take you home." Normally Helen would not have allowed herself to go into Harriot's carriage but when she stood, her legs buckled and she didn't have the strength to walk home.

"Thank you. I don't know how I can repay you." As she walked out, Harriot put her hand on Helen's arm and said, "We will be in touch. We are very sorry, Helen."

"Our cause just got personal," Helen heard Alice say as she left the foyer, exited the house and for the first time in her life stepped into a private carriage.

CHAPTER 4

Helen Comes Home

HELEN SAT IN HARRIOT'S carriage watching the streets fly by. The carriage wasn't moving fast enough, but nothing would be fast enough. She had to get home as soon as possible and see Abigail.

I'm sure she's home waiting for me. Will Albert be wondering where I am? Will he be saying: Why hasn't she started supper? I need to get home and see Albert! she thought, her mind racing. What WAS she doing in this private carriage? She still didn't understand how she ended up here. She sat straight up, not letting her back touch the cushioned wool seats and held onto the door handle to steady herself. She took a deep breath and didn't smell anything except the polished leather and her smoky sweaty smell. So different from the smells that normally assaulted her when she walked.

Everything was moving so fast: street signs, storefronts, pedestrians. Time. She wanted it all to stop. No, she really wanted to turn back the clock. She would place her body against the front door and block Abigail from going to work. Abigail! Abigail? Maybe she was alive and home waiting for her?

After what seemed like an interminable ride, the horse-drawn carriage finally pulled up in front of her tenement apartment. She didn't notice the stares from the people milling about the front of the building; the carriage was not a common sight in their neighborhood.

She stepped down, ignoring the driver's gloved hand for help and ran up the front stairs into the building as fast as her weak legs could take her. She walked into the apartment and stood in the doorway, looking around. Was Abigail sitting in the corner? It was dark in the apartment yet everyone's pale faces shone and stood out like the full moon on an inky black night. She waited for a moment for Abigail to run up to her, wrap her thin arms around her waist, give her a hug that wouldn't let go, and then tell her how she escaped the fire before it had gotten out of hand. She would smell the smoke on her but she would look at her face, take in her youth, her innocence and drink in her being there alive, healthy and untouched by the fire.

"Abigail? Abigail?" she called out.

"No Mama, Abigail's not here," Walter answered, her only son, 10 years old, his unsteady voice echoing in the small apartment. Her eyes settled to the dark apartment and she saw Iris sitting in a chair at the kitchen table. She was her neighbor, worked with her at the button factory and also Helen's closest friend.

"What are you doing here?" she asked with a quick tongue. They never visited each other's apartments until after supper and the children were settled: there was too much to do before then.

"Helen, Helen," Iris said softly. She stood up and walked towards Helen. She put her hand on Helen's elbow, attempting to get her to sit down, and Helen swatted it away immediately.

"Where's Papa?" she asked Walter.

"He went to bring her home," Walter answered afraid to say more.

"Bring her home?"

"Mama." Walter walked over to the doorway, where Helen

was still standing. He grabbed her hand, leading her to the chair at the kitchen table. "Mama, Abigail was in the fire." She let him lead her.

"I know. But maybe someone rescued her?"

"No Mama, she's not … she wasn't rescued …" his voice breaking.

"How do you know?" she screamed at him, watching him cringe.

"I was there with Papa. We went as soon as we heard about the fire. We saw her, Mama. They brought the bodies out. Papa sent me home. He's bringing her home." He then broke down and sobbed uncontrollably. Helen knew she should stand up, comfort him, put her arms around him, hug him hard. But she didn't move. She couldn't, and stayed seated in the chair, frozen. She couldn't comfort him. She saw Claudia come out from the darkness and rub Walter's back. Even though she was only eight years old, she was already playing the role of the caretaker in their family. Eleanor, at only four years old, and not understanding what was happening, came up to Helen's legs, her arms reaching up, wanting to be held. Helen ignored her—still frozen. Except for Walter's intermittent sobs, the apartment was deathly silent.

"It can't be true. It isn't true," Helen muttered.

Iris put her hand on Helen's shoulder and this time she allowed it. The two women remained silent, Iris standing behind Helen. Her hand felt heavier and heavier but the weight felt soothing. The only constant item that day that she understood. The fire. Waking up in Harriot's home. None of that made sense. She recognized Iris's scent: her castile soap mixed with perspiration and took comfort in it. Iris was devoted to her three young boys and always talked about how it broke her heart a little bit each day leaving them to work in the factory. The two women still didn't speak, but her friend's presence and soothing hand on the shoulder made the world stop spinning—momentarily.

"Why did I let her go to work?" Helen said so quietly only Iris could hear. Iris just squeezed her shoulder.

The apartment got darker as evening progressed; the doorknob turned and Albert walked in. They could smell the smoke from his clothing wafting inside as soon as he stepped in. Ashes like gray snowflakes clung to his coat. His boots were wet.

"Where is she?" Helen asked. Her voice sounded foreign in the taciturn apartment. Iris pulled her hand off her shoulder. Albert walked over to Helen, leaving his coat and boots on. He normally took them off straightaway. He stood over her and leaned into Helen to hug her. She burrowed her head into his wool coat.

"Albert, where is she? Albert, where is she? Where's our baby?" He was the only one who could hear her words, his coat muffling them to Iris, Walter, and the younger girls. He didn't answer. He pursed his lips and squeezed his eyes, holding back his own cries.

"She's only twelve. Who's going to take care of her?" He shook his head, unable to answer.

"We let her down. We were supposed to protect her. We didn't protect her." She couldn't finish. Her own guttural moans taking over, as she sobbed into his coat.

"I'm bringing her home, Helen," he finally said.

This isn't happening. Abigail is alive. She is. She'll walk through that door any minute now. She'll tell us stories about how she escaped and how scared she was. But she'll be back, Helen thought. She pulled herself away from Albert, stood up and walked into their only bedroom. Iris followed her.

"Let me help ya, Helen," and assisted taking off her outer clothing until she was just in her undergarments. Even though she and Albert normally slept on the couch in the living room, she collapsed on the bed in the bedroom, where all the children usually slept.

This wasn't how it was supposed to be. Abigail wasn't supposed to die before me. I was supposed to die first. How could this happen? she thought as she pulled the blanket over herself and cried herself to sleep. She just wanted to be alone.

CHAPTER 5

After the Funeral

IRIS HAD BEEN a godsend since the fire. She'd even collected a few days' wages from their co-workers at the button factory. Helen couldn't have prepared Abigail's body for burial without her. Iris used to say that she'd buried more siblings and cousins than she cared to remember. Once Abigail was brought back to the apartment, Iris walked in and started barking orders while Helen and Albert stood emotionally depleted.

"Claudia, put that blanket over her. She needs to stay warm."

"Albert. ALBERT! Grab some coal from the basement to heat the stove. We need warm water."

"Walter, collect some rags for washing."

"Ellie, come here. Give your Mama some room," and guided Eleanor from Helen's legs to attach to Iris's.

"Claudia, is there a bright dress we can use?"

"Yes, Abigail had a green one."

"Good. Get it for me."

Abigail's soldered clothing was soon a heap on the floor. Iris looked at Albert and said, "Take those to the incinerator, now." Helen stared at the pile.

When Iris left the apartment late that night, water was cleaned up from the floor, supper was heated on the stove and the children, Claudia, Walter, and Eleanor had been put to sleep in the bed in the only bedroom. Abigail was lying on the table, which had been moved from the kitchen area to near the front door.

"Tomorrow is another day. Try to get some sleep," Iris said and squeezed both Albert's and Helen's shoulders. As soon as the door closed, they looked at each other, Helen's body started shaking with sobs. They both fell to the floor, crumbled into the fetal position, intertwined with each other.

~

It had been a few short weeks since Abigail had died. Helen and Iris were walking home from their factory job: Helen had gone back a week after the funeral. They needed the money especially now that Abigail's paycheck was gone. She wasn't eager to go home after work, though, the smell of burnt skin and seared wood still lingered in the apartment. She was just going through the motions, sleeping fitfully, waking up in a sweat during the night, preparing meals for Albert and the children, getting everyone off to school and work and coming home to finish the day. Eleanor was being passed off from neighbor to neighbor, anyone who was free to watch her. She'd fall asleep on the sofa, not recalling how she got through the day. She and Albert had barely said ten words to each other since the funeral.

"Helen. Helen. Did you hear anything I said?" Iris waved her hand in front of Helen's face. Helen rubbed her eyes.

"Sorry Iris. What was that?"

"Have you been sleeping?" Iris asked.

"A few winks here and there," Helen responded and gave a half smile.

"Albert any better?"

"Nah. He's the same. But he's trying."

She heard a girl's voice on the street behind her; it sounded like Abigail: "Mama is this the block where Aunt Catherine lives?" and was startled by the 12-year-old adolescent pitch. When she turned, she saw a girl who looked nothing like Abigail.

~

"What's that carriage doing here?" Iris exclaimed. Outside the building a few neighborhood women stood clustered, pointing at a closed, polished black carriage. A uniformed man sat up front holding the reins of two well-groomed chestnut horses. Helen recognized it immediately: it belonged to Harriot Stanton Blatch.

"Would ya look at that carriage?"

"What's it doing here?"

"Fancy!"

"I'd like a ride in that."

Mrs. Blatch poked her head out the window, her small round eyeglasses peeking out from under a dark brown wool hat, pinned up on one side with a bow and with a short veil to her nose.

Iris let out a breath. "Oh she's beautiful. Small, but not thin, you know? Her face is so round. Like a china doll. Oh, Helen, look at her." Helen couldn't look away. It was like her heart had started beating again for just a moment when she saw that carriage.

"Mrs. Fox, are you available to take a ride?" Helen felt strangely pulled towards Mrs. Blatch; the warmth from the carriage felt magnetic, drawing her in. She glanced around, slightly nervous about the chatter, then she stepped inside.

"Mrs. Blatch, I'm surprised to see you .... here," she said, sitting straight up, her back not touching the seat. The air inside felt calm, clean, untouched by the grime and obtrusive noise hammering in her head all day.

"Mrs. Fox, dear," Mrs. Blatch reached out, while still leaning back against the seat, and put her hand over Helen's. Her hand was softer than any hand Helen had touched.

"The ladies and I were concerned about you and your family. We've been visiting many of the families affected by the fire in this neighborhood. I personally wanted to visit you and waited until after work hours. How are you faring?"

Did she really want to hear that she could barely speak without her eyes misting or that she woke up most mornings thinking it was a dream and was then shocked into the reality of what happened?

"We're keeping busy." Mrs. Blatch tapped the carriage and it started moving, at a slow pace.

"We are all tremendously distressed over the tragedy. I know your pain—I've lost loved ones tragically."

No one knew her pain. She stroked the nape of her heck. A few seconds later, Mrs. Blatch spoke up. "In fact, many of the ladies in our organization took up a collection, for the families," she held out a small velvet bag, coins shaking. "So many young girls—leaving families behind."

Helen shook her head, "I couldn't Mrs. Blatch, really I can't."

"I know dear, it's hard to accept this. But this is a simple gesture on our parts to show you how devastated we are by this tragedy and how we want to help you. The other families I visited felt the same way. But ... they ended up accepting our gift." They'd never accepted charity but, looking at the bag, she thought of the full meals they could have and the coal they could buy.

"You do not know us well yet, but we do not sit back and do nothing. The ladies of the League, and I, have to do something—for you—for the other families."

"The League?"

"The Equality League of Self-Supporting Women."

Helen raised her eyebrows.

"Suffragists," Mrs. Blatch continued. "We can't let a tragedy like the fire happen again. All those young girls working when they shouldn't have been. In such unsafe conditions ... if we could even vote, we'd have a choice of voting for politicians who would support our causes, keeping those young girls out of the factories, make the factories safer for the women working there. Now, I know how much this will help your family, I insist." Mrs. Blatch's voice was low yet firm as she placed the bag in Helen's hand.

Helen felt the warmth of Mrs. Blatch's hand as it touched her, and the sincerity of her smile. She wasn't sure why she closed her fingers around the bag, but it pushed against her fingers. *I don't want to upset her,* she thought. *But it's more,* whispered a voice deep in her head. The dizziness she'd felt in Mrs. Blatch's parlor all those weeks ago was hovering at the edge of her vision.

"Here we are," Mrs. Blatch said as they pulled up to Helen's building, having circled the block; landing like a ship docking back to shore.

"Helen, we can't bring your daughter back; however, there is a way we can prevent this from happening again." Mrs. Blatch paused and looked carefully at Helen. "We have a meeting next week at Cooper Union," she continued and placed a piece of paper in Helen's hand. "The details are on the flyer. Please think about it."

Helen stepped out of the carriage, looked at Mrs. Blatch, while holding up the velvet bag of coins, and said, "Thank you."

CHAPTER 6
Albert

ALBERT AND HELEN were barely making eye contact. The air in the apartment was stifling with a musty smell that got stronger as the days wore on. Abigail's death was gnawing at him and he had tried to talk to Helen on different occasions. She was dealing with her own grief but where did that leave him? She was reaching out: sideway glances, touching his shoulder, but that was it and it wasn't enough. Not his usual custom, that evening during dinner he declared and pushed himself away from the table, "I'm going out for a drink. Don't know when I'll be home." Heads around the table just nodded in acceptance. He headed out and was soon standing at the bar of McSorley's, not sure what to order. He wasn't a regular but had patronized from time to time.

"Albert, lemme buy ya a whiskey." Joseph, a man he barely knew, sauntered over. He nodded with his eyes misting at the familiar scents of sweet caramel and woody whiskey.

"How ya holding up?" another man asked. He nodded again, comforted by these acquaintances. The banter faded into the tobacco smoke above his head while the drinks warmed his body, nursing the gaping hole in his heart. He took a sip from his glass and realized he didn't want to be there, nor did he want to be home.

Albert sensed a slight trace of a feminine scent, looked up from his drink and noticed a woman standing next to him. She wore a full face of make up: pink cheeks, bright red lips, and darkened eyes. He had never seen a face like this up close: most of these women were in the theater or ladies of the night. Normally, there weren't many women in the taverns but maybe times were changing. She stood at the bar with her body fully turned to him, making him feel uncomfortable yet suddenly aroused in spite of himself.

"Honey, I heard about your ... tragedy," she whispered with a throaty voice. She wasn't touching him but was so close, ready to devour. Then, a tear rolled down her cheek and she grabbed a linen handkerchief from her bag to dab at her eye. The noises and sights in the tavern suddenly disappeared. He simply nodded, looking into her eyes. He had craved a connection like this with Helen.

"Honey, I haven't stopped thinking about your little girl. How can I help?"

He had let Abigail down when she went to work in the factory. He had let her down when she died. He had no idea how this woman could help.

"Honey ..." No one ever called him honey. It melted off her tongue, reached out, wet his lips and sent shivers down his spine.

"We buried my brother George last year at Calvary Cemetery on the other side of the river in Queens. He was just fourteen."

"What's your name?" Albert asked softly.

"Florence. How ya holding up?" she asked and put her hand on his arm, warming him up even through his shirt.

"Surviving," he answered.

"You sure you want to be seen talking to me?"

"I don't care about those dingbats. Can I walk you home?"

"You know what you're asking?" she asked with a smile.

He didn't; he just wanted to be alone with her, out in the fresh air. The smoke was getting to him.

"I don't think you can afford me," she added.

All of a sudden Albert understood what kind of woman Florence was. His judgment was clouded; he just wanted to be with her. He wanted to kiss her, to run his hands through her long wavy hair. He wanted to rub his face in her slightly revealing cleavage and envelope himself in her gardenia smell. The way she looked at him felt accepting, which wasn't what he was getting at home.

"You're right."

"Tell you what, I need to leave for a ... meeting. Why don't I drop you off at home? My carriage is right outside." She left through the back door without waiting.

Albert grabbed his coat from the chair; nearly toppling it over in his haste. Florence's carriage was positively opulent, the interior shielded by heavy velvet curtains. He parted them to find Florence wrapped in a heavy fur blanket. She smiled at him, patted the space next to her, then lifted the blanket to make room for him underneath. Finding courage, he didn't think he had, he leaned over and touched his lips to hers. Gently at first, but then hurried, sullied kisses that filled the intimacy void he had at home. He wanted to tear off her clothing and feel her naked body next to his. But he stopped himself and put his hands in his lap.

"That's a good idea. Let's bring you home and sleep on these hot feelings," she said, straightening her dress and tucking the loose hairs back in her chignon. Albert nodded, scratching his face.

"Drop me off here," he said. It was a few blocks from his apartment.

"I'll see you soon, Albert. After the winter, always comes spring," Florence said. He stepped out, never wanting her scent to leave him but eager to repair with Helen.

CHAPTER 7

May 1911. First Suffragist Meeting

"I WAS INVITED to a meeting tonight," Helen told Iris as they walked home from their factory down Bowery Street.

"You going out? After supper? What kind of meeting?" Iris asked, her eyes widened.

"A suffragist meeting," Helen answered, biting her bottom lip.

"Albert letting you go?" Iris asked. She didn't answer. "You haven't asked him yet, have you?" Iris stopped walking and turned to her,

"I'm going to ask him now. He'll say yes, don't ya think?" Helen asked.

Iris shook her head. "I don't know, Helen. We leave work, come home, make dinner, tend to the children," Iris answered. Helen bristled at the word "children." Iris stopped and put her hand on Helen's arm.

"I'm sorry," Iris said and they walked home in silence. As they approached their building, Iris turned to Helen and asked, "How important is this meeting? What kind of meeting is it again?"

"Suffragist." She saw the bewildered look on Iris's face. "Women getting the right to vote," Helen continued softly, hesitated for a moment and added, "It's important, I think."

"Then you have to talk to Albert," Iris said louder, linked her arm through Helen's and they marched up the stairs where their hungry children, spouses and dusty apartments waited.

~

Helen stood in the dim hallway outside her apartment door for a moment composing the courage to ask Albert's permission to go out and attend the meeting. Why was it so important to her? She knew it would be harder to ask since Albert had given up fighting for the unions at his factory. He claimed he didn't have the energy or motivation since Abigail died.

She remembered the suffragist parade that she, Abigail and Claudia had attended last year. They had been out on a Saturday doing the weekly shopping and had accidentally come upon the parade. Abigail had been transfixed by the hundreds of women, dressed in white dresses with banners representing their states and groups, marching down First Avenue, chanting "We NEED to Vote, We NEED to Work." Helen, in turn, had been captivated by Abigail's fervor.

Helen shook her fist, determined, opened the door, and called out "Hello, hello! Albert, children, Mama's home."

After supper, she put her hand's on Albert's shoulders while he sat at the table reading the late edition of *The Evening Standard*. She rubbed his neck, then said, "I was invited to a meeting—it's this evening."

Albert stiffened. "What kind of meeting?"

"Suffragist," she answered.

"What's that?" he asked, his voice raising.

"You remember. Those were the ladies that found me at the fire," Helen answered, seeing Albert's face fall. "It's for women getting the right to vote."

"Too risky, don't ya think Helen?" he said.

"Abigail didn't have a choice and had to work. Besides this was important to Abigail," Helen answered, clenching her jaw. "It was?" he asked.

"It was, and I want to learn more of what gave her such happiness, even for a brief time," She then told him about the parade they had accidentally attended the year before and how it had impacted Abigail.

Albert remained silent. He squeezed his eyes closed and said, "Seems pointless to me but go on."

"Thank you, Albert, thank you!" Helen said, and gave him a peck on his cheek. She rushed into the bedroom to look in the mirror, tuck in the loose hairs that had fallen out of her bun, tuck her shirt in tight to her skirt. She walked out of the apartment, energized, and called back, "Good night children, good night Albert."

~

Helen walked in late to the cavernous hall at Cooper Union. She looked around the vast space with just a few pieces of furniture and paused. So much space here and so little in it. The wood gleamed and she wondered how many women it took to keep it clean like that. She could barely keep the cobwebs out of the dark corners in her apartment.

Alice Paul was standing on stage, already speaking. Helen did remember meeting her at Harriot's home, the day of the fire, the day Abigail died. She couldn't recall if they had spoken, or what was Alice's role in the suffragist organization. She was surprised to see her commanding authority. Was she a leader like Harriot? The early evening light barely lit the room as the gas lights flickered. She saw an empty seat next to a lady dressed in a corseted silk dress but instead sat in the back of the room. Helen looked around at the hundreds of seated women; many in white outfits and sashes. She was overcome for a moment with thoughts of Abigail. Her mind flashed back again to the parade they stumbled upon months ago, walking back from the market. She'd been listening to Abigail chatter about this and that when they began to hear chanting and cheers. They rounded a corner and there was a wall of people. They had stumbled upon a large suffragist parade going up First Avenue.

Her daughter had been fascinated with the marchers. She had even talked of someday joining them. Standing in that immense hall, she was reminded. She had told Abigail in no uncertain terms she was not to get mixed up in that nonsense. It was too risky. But here she was, herself. If Abigail could see her now. Helen felt tears prick her eyes and she looked down for a moment.

She smelled their lilac perfume, listened to their polite clapping, watched them nod their heads and murmur in agreement and compared their tempered cheers with her rougher neighborhood. Her faded dark outfit accentuated how out of place she was. Her armpits felt damp with sweat.

When Mrs. Blatch had invited her, she knew she had to come. It was true, as she had told Albert, she wanted to understand more about the suffragists because Abigail had been so captivated. It also seemed that the suffragists had some power in preventing an accident like the fire happening again. She desperately needed a distraction to take her mind off the grief of Abigail's death. Perhaps, she had her own stirring of the suffragist cause at the parade?

"They said no one would join our cause. No one!" Alice Paul exclaimed. "Do you know how many women have signed up?" she asked the audience.

"Hundreds?"

"500?"

"1,000?"

"3,000?" the audience called out.

"No!!! 20,000!" The crowd erupted with applause. Hats fell

off heads, hands were clapping in the air and the floor shook with thunder. Helen found her own hands clapping alongside the crowd, caught up in the emotion.

"These are women from all walks of life. Educated, immigrants, Gramercy Park to Delancey Street."

Was Alice Paul telling the truth? Helen wondered. She looked around and was hard-pressed to see women like her, from her neighborhood. These women even smelled different; talcum powder wafted in the air. Wait, out of the corner of her eye, she spotted a small modest hat. Maybe there were women like her. She stood straighter and moved from the back of the room, a few inches closer to the heart of the crowd, feeling the heat of the audience and clapping her hands in unison.

"They don't want us to vote. They don't want us to make decisions that matter. How are we supposed to vote for the politicians we agree with? How are we supposed to protect our families? We can't do that if we don't have the right to vote!"

Helen's eyes misted. It was too late for Abigail. She felt a pit in her stomach, nauseous, and hoped she wouldn't throw up.

"We have a voice. We need to use it. They need to hear us! If not for us, then for our children!"

She thought about her children: Walter, Claudia and Eleanor. It wasn't too late for them. They could have choices, like these women. She couldn't leave now. She found herself merged with the group, adding her heat to the zeal of the crowd, not caring that she was sweating, that her hat was off her head, and was even tempted to roll up her sleeves. Her sweat smelling more feral as she hadn't bathed in over a week. As the meeting wrapped to a close, she felt a tap on her shoulder, turned around, and found herself face to face with Harriot Stanton Blatch.

"Mrs. Fox, do you have a few moments to speak before you leave?"

Helen nodded, she had already told Albert she would be late. She followed Harriot to a room in the back of the hall, feeling the air cool quickly as they walked away from the crowd. The chatter diminished and her ears popped from the quiet. The room was small, overstuffed after the nearly empty hall. Boxes, piles of signs and thick white ribbons were stacked to the ceiling. Mrs. Blatch immediately pulled out one of two chairs at a small table and sat down.

"What's all this?" Helen asked, her eyes darting.

"Pamphlets, flyers, banners and signs for our rallies and marches. Oohh I'm tired. These late nights are catching up to my old bones," Harriot sighed. "What did you think of the speeches tonight?"

Helen nodded her head with a small smile. "Alice Paul is tremendous. She really knows how to connect with women on every level. We are very fortunate to have her. You know she learned her Suffrage tactics in England with Emmeline Pankhurst?" Helen had no idea who she was but assumed someone famous the way Harriot seemed impressed. She continued, "We are in different parties: I founded the Equality League of Self-Supporting Women and Alice Paul has her Congressional Union. However, we have the same mission and work together all the time." She finally asked:

"Helen, we are looking for more women to get involved with the suffragist cause," Harriot paused. "More women like you."

"I would like to attend another meeting or rally," Helen said.

"That's not what I mean," Harriot continued.

"We need women on the ground—working with our organization."

"Why me?" Helen asked.

"I see a resilience in you. I was not sure if you were going to come. It would be a challenge for anyone to move forward after the tragedy you have been through. But here you are. I believe that they—the politicians, men—need to hear your story, from you."

Helen nodded. Was she ready to share her grief, her anger with the public? They needed to hear but would that even do anything?

"We need women from different parts of the city, such as your neighborhood."

Helen took a deep breath, squinting her eyes.

"You know Mrs. Fox, my mother, Elizabeth Cady Stanton who was one of the original suffragists with Susan B. Anthony, died very tired. She devoted her life to the movement, neglecting my siblings and me tremendously so. We wouldn't be as progressed if it weren't for her, but she did die tired." Harriot hesitated. "We are trying to do it differently and register as many women as we can, so that we can see this to the finish line. The cause truly needs women like you."

She continued, "What if your job and working for the suffragists were the same?"

Helen scrunched her face.

"The League is hiring—with a salary, we have the funds—so you can continue to get a paycheck. Why not devote your hard work to us instead?"

How much will she pay me? Helen thought, looking down at her worn boots.

"We can pay a weekly salary of $12," Harriot offered.

That's more than double what they pay me at the factory! Helen raised her eyebrows but kept it to herself. *What will Albert say when he finds out I'm making more than him?* she thought.

Was she really devoted to the suffragists? Or was this just an outlet for her to right the wrong of Abigail's death? What would Abigail even say about her mother working for the suffragists?

"Why don't you sleep on it? Come by the office in the next

few days and we can discuss more of the details. I'll be there every evening. Now, it's much later than usual and let's get us both home. Can I please drop you off with my carriage?"

Helen shook her head, finally able to speak. "Thank you, Mrs. Blatch. Thank you for your ... belief. I'll get myself home." She had a lot of thinking to do. What was Albert going to say to all this?

CHAPTER 8
May 1911

HELEN WOKE UP EARLY, surprisingly well-rested, with a clear head. Everyone was still sleeping. She had attended her first suffragist meeting a few nights before and couldn't stop thinking about Harriot's job offer. She stood up, pulled on her skirt over her nightdress to warm up. It fell down: she had less body mass to hold it up. Two months had passed since Abigail's funeral. She barely remembered any details; it was a blur. Iris and Claudia, now her elder daughter, had washed Abigail's body and prepared her for the funeral. Neighbors and friends from their respective factories had kept coming up to her, putting their hands on hers, patting her shoulder, trying to awkwardly hug her, asking her how she was faring, if she needed anything. But she stared back at them dry-eyed, barely nodding her head.

"How ya holding up Helen? If you want to talk ... my door's open," Iris would ask to Helen's silence as they walked home at the end of the day. Helen would nod and put her arm through Iris's. Their arms entwined tighter with each block.

That morning, though, the tightening in her chest abated. When did she eat last? She couldn't remember. She was now ravished. She ate a piece of cold bread with jam, not wanting to light the stove and wake up the family in their small apartment. She needed this quiet time.

"I can get some coal from the basement to light the stove," she heard Albert whisper.

"Why are you up so early?" she turned around and smiled at him. His face lit up in response. They had barely made eye contact since Abigail's death. She nodded her head.

"I'll get the coffee heated." Soon enough, they were sitting at the table, letting the smoke from the coffee fill their bodies. Helen reached out to touch his hand.

"How was your meeting a few nights back?" Albert asked. He had attended his own labor union meetings so she knew that he was genuinely interested. Even though she'd been honest about the suffragist meeting, she felt guilty for having an interest outside the family. She hadn't decided yet if she could accept the suffragist job Harriot had offered. If nothing else, the money was so tempting.

"Helen, there's something I need to tell you," he broached.

"Yes, Albert," feeling his hesitation. He walked up to his coat hanging on a hook by the front door and pulled out a handful of envelopes.

"I thought I could find the extra ... emptied the can ..." he put the envelopes on the table, not able to say more.

"What are these?" Helen asked, fingering the envelopes.

"Bills we owe."

"From what?"

"The funeral. We still owe the ... money," he said biting his lip.

"Oh Albert! Why didn't you tell me?" She looked down and saw his knee shaking. She put her hand on it to steady it. She then recalled how she had barely gotten out of bed after the funeral. It had been a whirlwind of activity. Neighbors that they barely had exchanged a word with, dropped off baked fish, creamed chipped beef, boiled potatoes, baked onions, cabbage salad. Boys, whose names they didn't even know, carted coal up to heat their stove and girls from other floors watched Eleanor so she wouldn't be a nuisance to her older siblings or Helen. A neighbor had dropped off a bag of coins that morning, "To help for the ... burial," and scurried out before Albert had had a chance to protest. Helen thought it had been enough to cover the expenses.

"I have something to tell you, too, Albert."

He looked up at her. Helen held her breath then got up. She went to the cupboard in the kitchen and grabbed a small dark blue velvet pouch. The coins inside clinked as she placed them on the table.

"Where'd ya get those?" Albert asked.

"Mrs. Blatch," Helen answered.

"Who's that?" Albert probed

"She's the head of the suffragist group. They were helping out all the families from the fire."

"Why'd you hold on to them? We needed them!" Albert said, slamming a fist on the table. He then fingered the pouch and put it in his shirt pocket.

"I thought the coins from the building were enough." Helen turned her face away from him and said softly, "Mrs. Blatch offered me a job to work for them."

"To do what?"

"Work in their office. Get more people from our neighborhood. I'd help with organizing marches, rallies, getting people from our neighborhood to come."

"You don't know how to do that or even work in an office," he said, drumming his fingers on his leg. Helen nodded her head.

"I can learn, Albert. I want to do this. These women—they want to help. They want to right the wrong that was done to Abigail. We have a choice here; one Abigail didn't have."

"I forbid this, Helen. We don't work in offices and we don't need any more of their help. Besides, what would the neighbors say?" Albert said. "This will be enough to take care of us," patting the pouch in his breast pocket.

"But Albert, they'll pay more. Much more than the factory," Helen said stroking her neck.

"We'll be fine, Helen. We don't need their help," he repeated. She slumped her shoulders and took a sip of her cold coffee.

CHAPTER 9

Abigail's Sweater

CLAUDIA WALKED INTO the kitchen, straightaway went to the stove and stirred the hot oatmeal for their breakfast. At eight years old, she was already helping with chores and filling in the void that Abigail had left. Helen looked at her.

"Claudia, put another sweater on. We have no money for doctors."

"None fit."

"Not now. Go in and grab a sweater."

"Mama, I looked, there weren't any sweaters in my size," she walked back into the bedroom and came out wearing a sweater.

"See Mama?" she said, tugging at the too-short sleeves and pulling it down to reach her waist. "I told ya, it's too small."

"There has to be one. Keep looking."

Claudia came out a few minutes later wearing a roomy mauve sweater.

"Mama, I found one. Better?" Claudia stammered.

Helen stood still. "Take that off. Now."

"But Mama, you said—"

"I said, take it off," Helen said through clenched teeth, her pitch neutral. The bustle of the breakfast routine stopped immediately and everyone stared at Claudia. She fought back tears and took the sweater off. Helen knew she was being unreasonable and everyone was walking on eggshells around her. There was no reason Claudia shouldn't wear Abigail's sweater.

"Not so fast. Ya just said she needs a sweater," Albert said standing up.

"That's not her sweater," Helen pushed an imaginary hair out of her face and looked away.

Not now Albert. Not now.

"C'mon Helen. You're being unreasonable. Let the girl wear the sweater. It's frigid out, you're shivering."

I see Abigail in that sweater. She wore it days before, maybe months before ....

"I'm not ready."

"We don't have a choice, god dammit. The girl's growing and it's cold. We can't buy a new one. You know that. Enough."

I CAN buy her a new one if I take this job.

"There's gotta be another one. Let me look," she said and dashed into the bedroom rummaging through the dresser, only finding Abigail's sweaters. She grabbed one and put her face in it, desperate to inhale Abigail's smell. She couldn't smell her anymore; it just smelled like the rest of them now. She walked back into the kitchen, head down, and started to clean up the breakfast dishes.

"Helen." Silence.

"Helen! Look at me." Silence.

"Let her wear the sweater." Silence.

I can't talk. I miss Abigail so much my stomach hurts, my chest tightens when I go to sleep. He has no idea how I feel. Why did I let her work in the factory?

"I'm not ready," she whispered.

"What?"

"I'm not ready to hand over Abigail's ...."

"None of us are ready. But ... we've got to live our lives.

Abigail would want that."

"How do you know what Abigail would want?" Helen snarled. Albert's body became rigid, she heard a small gasp. Her heart fell even deeper, knowing she was hurting him. He had done nothing wrong. In fact, he was just trying to make her happy with small efforts: offers to rub her feet at night, fetching water from the spout downstairs. She rebuffed him at every turn. He didn't know the guilt she felt for letting her daughter leave school and go to work. She looked at him, really looked at him for the first time in—she couldn't even remember. His face was pained, brows furrowed so deep, he seemed to have aged overnight.

"I don't want us to forget about her," she whispered

"We're never gonna."

"Yes, we will. We have to keep her clothing separate."

"We're not living, Helen. We're ghosts hovering around, afraid to touch, not talking. I know my Abigail. She would've yelled at us long ago. We still have this," he pointed to Claudia, Walter towering over her, and Eleanor barely reaching table height. They were all staring at Helen. She had forgotten they were there. She needed to pay more attention to them. Was that a bruise on Eleanor's chin? How did it get there?

"We still have each other," he said and reached out to grab her shoulder. She flinched at the warm touch of his hand and he immediately retracted.

"You're not the only one who feels her gone." He stopped and looked around. "Everything reminds me of her ... when I tie my boots in the morning, she'd say 'Don't forget your flat cap Papa.' Or she was always singing to the little ones when she'd tuck them in at night, you remember ... we all miss her, Helen. But, we're still here. Come back to the living," he took a handkerchief out of his pocket and blew his nose. He then grabbed his lunch box, woolen sweater hanging over the chair, and stormed out of the apartment.

Helen stood still, afraid to move. She felt the children's eyes pore into her. She just wanted to get dressed and go to work, even if it was the factory. She wouldn't have to think there. But she did look at her children.

Walter tiptoed over to her, "Mama?"

She pulled him close to her, he seemed to have grown inches and reached her head, now 11 years old. Claudia wasn't even fighting back her tears anymore; they were streaming down her cheeks, leaving a mark on her unwashed face. When had the children bathed last? She looked at all three of her children again. She didn't have a choice: she had to work with the suffragists. They would make it better. Yet, how would she move forward and still hold on to Abigail's memory?

CHAPTER 10

Walter

HELEN SAT ON THE BED in the bedroom tallying the money in the can. After buying coal and paying the rent, they only had $1.43 left for food for the rest of the month. Neighbors had stopped dropping off meals. She muttered to herself tearfully, "Abigail's pay would've helped right now," then swallowed hard over the statement. She walked into the kitchen to start supper and saw Albert and Walter sitting at the table. Walter's eyes gazed downward and Albert was whispering in his ear. She placed a few handfuls of lima beans with lard in a pan on the lit fire on the stove to cook for dinner. As she grabbed a potato to peel, Albert called to her, "Helen, we need you."

"Not now. Supper needs fixing."

"It can wait. Claudia, go take over for your mother." Claudia ran up without a word and took over peeling the potatoes.

Helen sat down and sighed.

"I told Walter that we'd registered him for school again."

"Mama, I can't go!"

"Walter, you're going," Helen said while looking at him with knitted brows.

"I want to work in a factory. Like Papa. I hate school."

"Walter, you have to stay out of the factories. Learn a trade. Maybe even graduate?" Helen said. She took off her sweater and sat upright. This discussion was going to go very differently than the one they had had with Abigail when she defied her parents and went to work despite Helen's and Albert's protests.

"WHAT? No one we know has a high school diploma. That's so long aways." He was right but she didn't care.

"Mama, I'm behind the other boys in class," he stammered.

"I'll talk with Samuel's mother on the 4th floor, he's in your class. Maybe he can share his studies."

"Aww who cares. I already know my arithmetic and how to read. What else do I need to learn?" Walter said as he lifted his chin slightly and brushed his hair away from his eyes and forehead. "Besides, who's going to bring in Abigail's money?"

Helen looked at Albert. "I could take that job."

Albert blinked his eyes at her, "We decided you weren't working there."

Helen stood up, her chair nearly falling over, marched to the closet in the bedroom and grabbed the can. She slammed it on the kitchen table. "We have $1.43 left this month to buy food for a family of 6." She wiped her nose with the back of her hand. "Family of 5 now." She pointed at Walter. "Do you want him to work? We can't let this be the fate of our children." Albert said to Walter, "Go join your sisters on the sofa."

Albert looked at Helen. "I can't have my wife working—what in an office?"

Helen leaned forward and looked in Albert's eyes, "We don't have much Albert, but I—we can do this for our children." She broke down crying, "I let Abigail down. We let her down. We never should have let her work there."

Albert leaned over and hugged her tight. "I know. I wish we had never let her go either," starting to weep himself.

"I just feel so guilty. But we can do something now. Please Albert, let me work for the suffragists. We need the money. It'll keep Walter in school. Please?"

Albert's silence signified defeat. He simply nodded his head over and over in the crook of her neck. Abigail's death loomed large in the room and was too hard to fight against. Walter was going back to school and Helen was going to work for the suffragists.

CHAPTER 11
New Job

HELEN LOOKED AT THE crumbled piece of paper in her hand, barely making out the address Mrs. Blatch had written. She had folded and unfolded it so many times, the address was nearly faded, but she had memorized it.

She found the building and saw a small sign outside: "Equality League of Self-Supporting Women." She was in the right place. She wasn't as familiar with this part of town, Gramercy Park: the brownstone houses fitting close together instead of the heavy tenement buildings in her neighborhood. The sidewalks had tall, well-maintained trees and each brownstone had vibrant potted flowers in front. The air was less smoky, being far from the factories downtown near her home. She smoothed her skirt, dusted her hands off, adjusted her hat and walked in through the front door. As she fingered the few coins in her pocket, she thought about the $12 weekly salary Mrs. Blatch had offered with this new job. Double what she was making!

Standing in the hallway, she heard voices right away, immediately sounding different than her neighborhood: full sentences crisply spoken out, strong voices not yelling, but speaking with authority.

"I don't think we should go back uptown to 57th Street.

We've rallied on multiple street corners and don't want to repel the women in that neighborhood. We need to find a new area to canvas."

"That's not the case! Those women are just getting to know us. They'll bring their friends, their neighbors."

"We need new signatures ...."

Helen's jaw gaped but she glanced away, nervous to make eye contact.

Many women walked around, a few stood in groups talking to each other, and others sat on a sofa looking at sheets of paper together. She hadn't thought it would be so busy. They were all dressed smartly yet not too ostentatious. There were heavy wooden desks and writing tables with ornate wooden chairs to match all laid on lavish Persian rugs. Helen startled at the sight of tall plants in the corners. A plant inside? What a thing.

No one looked at her and she didn't see Mrs. Blatch. She just stood there. Finally, someone looked up and asked, "May I assist you?"

"I'm here to see Mrs. Blatch."

"Whom? Please speak up."

Helen cleared her throat, "I'm here to see Mrs. Blatch," speaking louder.

"She's in the back. Whom may I say is calling?"

"Hel ... Mrs. Fox."

A few moments later, Mrs. Blatch came out, "Mrs. Fox. I'm delighted you are here." She grabbed Helen by both hands and led her to an office in the back. Mrs. Blatch motioned to a chair at a small table and they both sat down.

"Tell me dear, tell me. Have you decided to join the cause?"

Helen didn't answer right away. She had not expected to start the conversation so quickly.

Finally, she stammered, "I've thought about it. Plenty. Mrs. Blatch ...."

"Yes?"

"Well, you may not know but …."

"Yes dear. You can share with me."

"Well, I need to work. You can really pay $12?" Mrs. Blatch then smiled. Helen felt her skin itch and her cheeks warm.

"We know that! Of course, you need to work. We've gotten donations supporting our cause and can afford that. It could be even more later on. Will it be enough?"

Helen's eyes widened. Was she serious?

"We really need the additional support, dear. We have so many marches and rallies to plan!"

"Oh … I haven't been to many marches and rallies."

"We know. We didn't expect that. As I might have mentioned, we need to enroll more working women, from different neighborhoods. We would teach you our current methods. They work wonders—the Pankhurst method—we just need more persons involved. Is this something that you would be interested in?"

Helen's eyes widened, still in disbelief, but she smiled.

"Have you spoken to your husband about this?" Mrs. Blatch asked.

"Albert?"

"Yes, Albert." Helen nodded.

"He gave his permission?" Helen nodded again and said softly, "I would like to work with you. Work with the suffragists."

"That's wonderful news, dear!" Mrs. Blatch clasped Helen's hands. They felt especially tender compared to her red chapped ones. "Why don't we start tomorrow. See you here at 9am?"

As Helen walked out of the office and onto the street, she smiled to herself and then felt a panic pang wondering how she would talk about her new job to Albert and Abigail. Oh, Abigail! Had she really forgotten that Abigail had died?

CHAPTER 12

First Paycheck

IT WAS LATE, they were normally asleep at this time, but Helen and Albert lay wide awake on their bed, the sofa in the main room. They had the windows open to cool down the apartment from the early summer heat of the day.

"Tell me again how much they paid you," Albert whispered stroking Helen's hand. She was holding the dollar bills she had just received from her first week working at the suffragist office.

"I told ya. 12 dollar bills."

"We never get dollar bills—just coins. You can go to the butcher tomorrow. We can finally have some meat for supper."

Helen concurred. She thought about the hole in the sole of her boot and the shoe store near the butcher. Maybe the next time she got paid.

"What is it?" she asked, hearing his stomach grumble.

"I can taste the lamb you'll make tomorrow. Use Mama's recipe?"

"Ya, with potatoes and apples."

"Do you think the neighbors will notice we're spending more?" Albert asked. Helen shrugged her shoulders.

Albert sighed and continued. "I feel—guilty, for being excited about the meal knowing that Abigail won't be here."

"Did we let her go to work too easily? Remember when she came to us and told us about the job?" Helen asked.

"Helen, we barely had enough for food," Albert reminded her. "Besides, other girls in the building were going to the factories, too."

"We didn't even put up a fight. Not every family sent their twelve-year-old daughter to the factories." It almost seemed Abigail was in the room with them while they were talking. Helen half expected her to look at them and say, *It's ok Mama. I wanted to go to work. You had told me what a big girl I was helping our family out.*

"I know, Albert. I know," Helen said as tears rolled down her cheek and she fingered the dollar bills, then put them back in the velvet pouch Harriot had given her in their first carriage ride together.

"I never woulda thought when we moved here from the farm, with just Abigail in tow, that she wouldn't be here with us. Is this what we thought about creating a better life?" Albert asked.

The year was 1899. Helen and Albert had been married just a year, even though they had known each other since they were young children, having grown up together in their small farming town in the northern west area of New York, near Seneca Falls. Abigail had just been born. Helen and Albert had stayed up late one night talking.

"I just don't think we can last another winter here, Helen."

"What are you saying Albert?"

"Pa and I counted the crops for the year. It's the third year in a row that we are short."

Helen wasn't surprised about the comment. They had all been pitching in, her Mama watching Abigail while she helped the boys in the field, but the meals were sparse and the smiles few to spare.

"I got a letter from John. He said the city is better than they thought." John was Albert's cousin. More like a brother.

"It'll break Mama's heart not to watch Abigail. She and Papa can't leave the farm and come with us. And she's got my brothers to look after. Would we even have room for her in New York?"

"What else can we do, Helen? Don't we want a better life?" She remembered leaning inward and fidgeting in her chair. Were they really going to move to New York City?

Now it was twelve years later and they were in New York City. Night and mornings were especially hard since Abigail died.

"Good night Albert, let's try and get some sleep. Staying up all night isn't going to do anything for us."

∼

Helen's hands trembled slightly as she put her gloves on as she walked out of the building, heading to the suffragist office for her second week of work. She smoothed down her brown tweed skirt and tucked in a loose hair that had fallen out from her tight bun, then skipped a few steps on the landing.

She walked into the office, took off her coat and heard, "Helen, come join us, we need you to plan our next rally," Harriot said. Harriot was seated on the couch with Alice Paul. Helen sat next to Harriot, not ready yet to make eye contact with Alice.

"How come you plan so many rallies?" Helen asked, her eyes downward.

Alice looked at her and asked. "How did you first hear about the suffragists, Helen—Mrs. Fox?"

"Well, uh," she started to stammer. "I came upon a parade suddenly with my daughter— my daughters."

"Exactly! We need to reach women from all the neighborhoods, uptown and downtown."

Harriot put her hand on Helen's arm, "Helen dear, the laws that are passed affect us women as much as they affect men. Yet we have no say in voting for the lawmakers who pass those laws. Doesn't seem fair, does it?" she said shaking her head with a smile. Helen shook her head back.

"And ... these laws affect our children. Wouldn't you agree that these lawmakers should have the woman's point of view?" Helen nodded, feeling her eyes mist.

"Did you know there are over 8 million women earning wages in the United States?"

Helen opened her mouth.

"It is our duty to protect and elevate those women!" Harriot said shaking her fist.

"Yes! Yes!" Helen cried out.

"You know, Helen, I'm not as young as you or these other women," Harriot said waving her hand at other women in the office. "I'm counting on your vigor."

"You can count on me, Mrs. Blatch. Please, tell me what I can do for this next rally. Let me grab a pencil and paper to take notes."

"For starters, we want to make sure we have all the permits we need from city hall. I don't believe the police will give us a hard time any longer. They used to ban our rallies but seem to leave us alone for now. Let's make flyers to hand out and announce it." Harriot continued with the details and Helen wrote them down furiously.

"Now I need to get ready for my lunch with Mrs. Alva Belmont. Helen, you'll be able to hand out the flyers to the women in your neighborhood?" Harriot asked and stood up.

"Of course, Mrs. Blatch, I won't let you down!"

"Please dear, call me Harriot. We are now on the same team."

How on earth will I hand out these flyers to the women in my building and old factory? They will truly think I have lost my mind,

Helen thought as she stood and moved to her desk to start working on the rally.

CHAPTER 13

Working With Suffragists. November 1912

"IRIS, IRIS," Helen called out. Iris was in front of her going down the stairs. She stopped but didn't turn around right away. Albert and the children were still eating breakfast but Helen was leaving earlier than normal that day.

"I'm so happy to see you, to run into you," Helen said a little louder than normal. Iris turned just her head around.

"Yas, it's been a few weeks," she responded, slumping over slightly.

"Oh Iris. I've been meaning to stop by but I get home from— my office—later these days and then need to help Claudia prepare supper," Helen answered, coughing into her gloved hand. "I promise to stop by one evening,"

"Not too late, though," Iris said.

"Of course not," Helen responded. As they got to the street, Helen looked at Iris and leaned in to touch her shoulder. "I have to go this way," pointing uptown. Iris nodded and started to head downtown to the factory where they used to work together. She turned back to look at Helen.

"How ya feeling, Helen? Abigail's been gone so long now," she asked, squinting her eyes. Helen took a deep breath. How would she answer her? It had been almost two years but still felt like yesterday. She couldn't admit that working for the suffragists distracted her enough to forget the pain, forget Abigail had died. In fact, she was swept up in the euphoria at the office: the influential women, their powerful connections, and persuasive speeches. She had been with the suffragists nearly a year and a half!

"Mornings and nights are toughest. I wake up sometimes thinking it was a bad dream," Helen answered. Iris squeezed her arm and turned around to head to her factory.

Helen walked up to the suffragist NAWSA office on Waverly Place. She stopped for a moment outside and fingered the small brass sign hanging outside: National American Woman Suffrage Association. She opened the door, hung up her hat and coat on the rack, surprised to see other hats and a Victorian cape coat with fur collar already hanging; she wasn't the first one in the office. Her small boater hat with its flat brim looked plain hanging next to the broad flower pot hat with three-story height.

"Helen, good you are here. Come, come. I was just starting to tell Alice about the rally we've been planning!" Harriot called from the formal sitting area.

The two women sat facing each other on upholstered couches. Helen pulled up a chair slightly behind Alice, her feet sinking into the plush rug. She had been spending more time working with Alice, with Harriot's permission. The different parties were confusing but Harriot and Alice were so close and kept reiterating that they were fighting the same cause.

"Helen, thank you for responding to the reporter from The Sun. They've been relentless in following my every move ever since I returned from England," Alice said.

"What are they afraid of?" Helen asked, blushing with Alice's acknowledgment.

"Perhaps that I'll break store windows or handcuff myself to a railing?" Alice said with a slight smile. Helen tilted her head.

"Don't worry, Helen. I don't plan on doing those tactics here—for now." Alice reassured her.

"That's enough, Alice. Don't frighten the poor girl. She just started and we don't want her running out of here scared to her wits," Harriot admonished.

Helen sat up straighter in her chair and crossed her arms in front of her body.

"Now let's discuss the project I have in mind." Helen turned to face Harriot. "We need to get our message out in a more drastic manner. Our previous attempts have not been strong enough. I want lawmakers up in Albany to know we mean business. We need to keep the attention focused on women and I have a new idea. I'm proposing that we march from New York City to Albany—walking the entire way—over three days," Harriot said, moving her hands around.

Walk all the way to Albany? In the snow and cold? Albert will never let me go. I've never even left New York City since we moved here, Helen thought.

"Can these women handle marching in the snow and cold?" Helen asked.

"Of course! We are hearty and determined. Look how many are showing up to our open-air meetings in Cooper Union, parks and other areas in the city," Harriot answered.

"Harriot, with all due respect, open air meetings are much different than a multi-day march from New York to Albany," Alice retorted. She pressed down her palms on her lap and smoothed her skirt towards her knees a few times. Her boot heels were off the ground raised and she was on her toes, even though she was sitting down, as if ready to pounce. "I'm a proponent of drastic sacrifices, that's what I learned in England; but I need to focus on a bigger event for the spring. President-elect Wilson's inauguration is in March and we need to take advantage of this monumental happening. What can we plan that truly gets their attention?"

She's talking about the President like he's her friend. Even in the paper, he seems bigger than God. I want to side with Harriot—she's been so true to me and helped me. But, Alice has a point. The inauguration seems important. She watched the two women stare at each other, their lips pursed. Helen held her breath, afraid if she said anything that they would both turn on her.

"What exactly do you have in mind for the inauguration?" Harriot asked.

Alice shook her head, "I don't know yet. Wilson has been playing with our group, offering support at arm's length but not taking any strident actions. I want to carefully plan an event that will be impressive and prompt results. I need to be thoughtful about this and not rush."

"Alice, I agree that we need to take advantage of the inauguration next March. But it's only November and there is so much we can do in the meantime. We will get to that," Harriot stared at Alice unblinking. She then turned to Helen.

"Helen, let's get the updated list of women who we think will join us on our march from New York to Albany. We need a list of supplies we will need so we can start organizing and collecting." Helen dutifully reached for a pencil and paper from a nearby desk to begin the list. She held her pencil in mid-air and sat up.

"I saw a full bag of mail by the front door. There might be letters from more women wanting to help."

Alice looked over at the mail bag. "It does look fuller than last week."

"Oh yes. We are getting more letters from women wanting to volunteer and sending in donations. Just last week, we received $173!"

"I had no idea! That's more than we've received in weeks,"

Harriot said and clapped her hands.

Helen stood up, went to the desk she was using against the wall, turned on the colored glass lamp and shuffled through papers. She found one, held it up, and said, "I'm listing all the women who mailed us from the last month. I'll post back to them and invite them to this march to Albany."

"Well done, Helen, well done!" Alice said. Helen looked at Harriot waiting for a reaction as well. Harriot sat with her fingers in a steeple and smiled at Helen, proud of her protege.

"Yes, Helen, well done."

A maid appeared and poured three cups of steaming tea. Helen didn't touch it; not comfortable yet to be waited on.

CHAPTER 14

Working Late

HELEN SHOOK HER WRIST to get the aches out of her fingers. She had been writing names onto a list all day from the outpouring of letters they were receiving daily. She felt a presence over her shoulder.

"That's a long list of women, Helen!" Alice exclaimed. Helen turned her head around suddenly.

"Goodness, what time is it?" she asked, noticing the darkness.

"It's nearly 7:30pm. We're the last ones in the office. I've seen the mail bags arrive but had no idea it was this many," Alice said.

"I've started writing them back and reaching out to join the march next month from NYC to Albany," she said, then added as she stood up, "I've got to get home, Alice. I've lost track of time!"

Alice put a hand on her arm. "Helen, I know Harriot brought you into our organization." Helen looked at her directly. Alice continued, "Harriot feels strongly about the Albany march next month, wanting to work on our New York politicians. I do agree with her. You've been instrumental in persuading women to join a march outside in cold December. I'm impressed with the number that have volunteered so far.

But we need more."

Helen rubbed her chin and chewed her lip. "More names for the march to Albany?" Helen asked.

"No. Bigger! We're going to Washington next year for our own suffragist parade before Wilson's inauguration."

"Oh, yes—I heard you mention that to Harriot."

Alice reached over and touched the multiple sheets of paper with women's names and addresses, some even had phone numbers listed. "This list is phenomenal for us to reach these women for the Washington parade." Helen nodded in agreement.

"Good job, Helen. I'm counting on you to help me make this an even grander success!" Alice said.

"Thank you, Alice. I have to run home now and get supper going."

"Rest up, Helen. General Jones is coming in tomorrow."

"General Jones?" she asked, raising her brows.

"You won't be disappointed, she's a spitfire! I have donor letters to write and will see you tomorrow. Good night, Helen," she said, sat down at her desk and looked down at her papers.

Helen walked into the apartment ready for the barrage of anger over her late arrival. She found her family sitting at the table already eating supper. She quietly took her coat and hat off and hung them by the hooks near the front door. Eleanor ran to her and hugged her tight in the waist.

"Mama, Mama! We were so hungry and started without you," she looked up at Helen's face.

"Oh honey, that's fine. I understand. Mmmm, smells good. What did you cook?" she asked, looking at Claudia.

"I heated up the stew from last night and added beets from the storage area in the basement." Helen smiled but felt like pouting. She looked at Albert, his lips pressed together in a firm line, the pomade still stiff in his hair from the morning and his shirt half tucked in. She walked over and turned up the gas light to brighten up the apartment and sat down at the table.

Later that evening, as she was changing into her night-clothes, she felt Albert's eyes on her. A lock of his hair had fallen into his eyes. He ran his hands through his hair to put in back into place.

"You're different, Helen."

"What do you mean?"

"Look at that blue skirt. I don't even recognize it."

"Oh that." Helen waited a moment. "One of the ladies in the office gave it to me. It didn't fit her anymore." *That wasn't true. It still fit her but it was last year's fashion and Violet from the office wouldn't wear it anymore,* Helen thought.

"It's not the skirt, Helen!"

"Albert, what is it?"

"I heard you humming."

"Humming?"

"Yas, when you were washing the dishes after supper."

Helen hadn't even realized she was humming. She had been thinking about Alice's compliment at the end of the day. "I had— I had—something good happened to me at work today," Helen shared, her chin trembling. "I got—Alice Paul told me I was doing a great job."

Albert looked at her puzzled.

"No one's ever spoken to me like that."

Albert bowed his head. "Don't you miss her Helen?" he asked quietly. All of a sudden, Albert seemed softer, the room seemed warmer, she moved closer to him.

"Albert, of course I do! I miss her every waking moment. Every breath I take, I miss my baby."

"You just seem sometimes like you've forgotten. Forgetting us, even."

"Oh, Albert. I'll never forget her. I couldn't do this without you," she leaned in to hug him tight, hoping he would feel her body's warmth through the thin layer of her nightclothes. Feel her breasts pressed against his chest. She would show him how much she didn't forget about him. How much she loved him.

CHAPTER 15

General Jones

"HELEN, DID VIOLA show you how to print the flyers on the offset press so we can hand them out at tomorrow's rally? We ran out so quickly after yesterday's meeting."

"Yes, she did. I already did them, Alice."

"Good. I'm glad you aren't calling me Miss Paul." After she and Alice had worked late at the office a few times together, they were now on a first name basis.

"Alice," Helen said, biting her nail.

"Yes, Helen?"

"The rally tomorrow is near the tenements."

"Yes."

"That's where I live."

"I know."

"I don't think the ladies in my neighborhood will make this March to Albany."

"Don't they see how important it is to convince the lawmakers in their own offices?"

"Yes, but they can't take days off work or leave their children untended."

"Oh. I see," Alice said. "Perhaps they will be inspired by our speakers?"

"I don't think so, Alice." Alice now raised her brows.

Did I insult her? If I don't say anything, she'll never find out what the women in my neighborhood really need, Helen thought.

"The speakers are good but these women need to keep their families fed and safe," Helen continued.

"The speakers will talk about safety in the factories," Alice said.

"Yes Alice. But if we want the women to support us with the right to vote, we also don't want to anger their husbands," Helen said.

"Oh, I see."

"Their husbands won't like these women leaving the home for more than work," Helen said.

"What do you suggest?" Alice asked.

"If the speakers can convince them that voting will lead to higher wages, these women may be convinced *and* not anger their husbands."

"That's a good point, Helen. Let me make sure the speakers talk about safety in the factories *and* that with the power to vote they can help pass laws for higher wages! They can't do that now."

Helen's smile reached her eyes, feeling more relaxed.

Next time, I'll tell her we have to work, we don't have a choice, she thought, and walked over to Harriot to continue the work on the march from NYC to Albany.

∼

"General Jones is going to be here any moment. Do you have more sheets of women that can march to Albany?" Harriot asked.

"Right here, Harriot. It keeps growing." She gave her three sheets of paper with nearly 100 names of women and their addresses. She had stayed late three nights in the last week writing them down from the letters that kept multiplying daily.

She felt energized from the pressure to finish this essential task, but the icy tones she got from Albert when she came home late, together with the guilt she felt not coming home early for her family, dampened the exhilaration.

Helen was helping a great deal to prepare for the Albany march: arranging for homes where the ladies who were marching could stay along the route and making copies of pamphlets the marchers could give out along their route. She relished the responsibility. As a result, Alice Paul seemed to accept her more, including her in more conversations and giving her more tasks. Helen was eager for her approval and drawn to her magnetic authority. She would do anything to chip away at Alice's reserved demeanor and change her opinion of her.

"You've done a great job gathering these women for the march," Harriot said, scanning the list of names. Helen let out a nervous laugh which caused Harriot to fix her gaze on her.

"What is it, Helen?"

"I don't think I can be part of this march."

"But you are, dear! You've played a tremendous role," Harriot said leaning forward.

"That's not what I mean. I can't join the march. I've never left New York City."

"Well this will be a great opportunity!"

"It's more than that," Helen said crossing her arms.

"Yes?"

"I can't leave my family and," Helen looked away, "Albert will never let me."

"Oh, I see," Harriot said nodding impatiently.

"It's just not possible. I am eager to meet General Jones, though," she added.

"You won't be disappointed, she's a fiery one!"

"How did she get her name 'General'? Are women allowed to be in the army?"

Harriot laughed and Helen felt her cheeks redden. "No,

dear. That's our next battle. Her real name is Rosalie Gardiner Jones, of the Oyster Bay socialites."

Helen cocked her head.

"When I saw her at the Long Island benefit in October, she came up with the idea of the hike from New York to Albany and then offered to organize it. Her family is very connected, especially to the press. Next thing you know, the papers nicknamed her the 'General' and it's been in the papers nonstop. You could say she has a louder than average voice."

Helen now knew that "very connected" meant wealthy.

The front door flew open, and the strong wind pushed it to bang against the wall.

"Harriot, Harriot, you've got to see this list of reporters I've put together. I promise you they'll be there next week when we take off on our hike." General Jones marched into the sitting room. She hadn't even stopped to take off her Crown blue Toque hat and stood right in front of Helen, who felt the spit drops on her face.

General Jones stopped talking for a moment, then looked directly at Helen: "Who the hell are you?"

~

Helen and Iris sat in Iris's apartment, two floors above hers. Helen wrapped the shawl around her tighter while watching Iris iron her husband's shirts. The heat from the iron was warding off the chill of the December air. The temperature had dropped and frost pushed through the windows. The wind moaned and on her way home, Helen saw leaves and pieces of trash blowing around in cylinder circles.

It was after supper; the children were all asleep and Albert was reading the paper, giving Helen a window to visit with her friend. She found herself holding back and not telling Albert all the upbeat happenings of her work day. They were finally in a better place.

"And then when General Jones asked who I was, Harriot pointed to me and said, 'That's Helen Fox. She's our hardest worker here. This march to Albany won't happen without her!' I wish I could go."

"That's great to hear, Helen," Iris stopped ironing for a moment. "You would go on a trip?"

"It's a trip but it's part of my job. I've been working so hard putting it together."

"Albert would never let you," Iris went back to her ironing. Helen tapped her foot.

"Tell me, how are the children doing?" Iris asked and took the cast iron back to the stove to reheat. Helen knew she was happy for her but felt the divide widen. She walked down the flight of stairs slowly to her apartment and resolved the next morning to bring up the march to Albert. *He could be reasonable, couldn't he?* She thought, feeling a glimmer of possibility.

CHAPTER 16
March to Albany

"GENERAL JONES, are you joining the women on the hike?" the reporter from the New York Daily asked. Helen watched the diamond ring on the General's puffy finger glisten as she waved it around, catching rays from the snow banks on the sidewalk.

"Of course! Wouldn't miss it for the world!"

The General spoke like everyone was going on the hike from NYC to Albany. *Did she have any idea that not everyone had options?* Helen thought, clenching her fist.

Helen had been on a roller coaster of anger and excitement these last few weeks. She kept looking for opportune moments to bring up the march with Albert, but it never seemed like the right time. She didn't have the argument nor strength that would convince him. She would be at the office elated and ready to join the women marching. Then she would go home at the end of the day and her resolve would dissolve as soon as she walked through the door. She also wasn't sure if she was ready to leave her children. Would she ever be ready?

Helen looked around at the women gathered at the IRT subway station on 242nd Street in the Bronx, the starting point for the March to Albany. As she had told Alice, no one from her neighborhood ended up part of this crowd. It was an especially frigid day in December 1912 and she watched the fat snowflakes fall down on their thick wool suits, tawny brown fur coats and large velvet hats. With tight lips, she could smell the wet fur, standing so close yet feeling an ocean apart. They were prepared for the cold, whereby she stood on the cold cement sidewalk feeling the wind cut through her threadbare coat and thin sweater. She stomped her feet to warm up, the cold shivers running up and down her legs. Did these women have any idea that every cent she earned made a difference between cold and heat? She took a deep breath and blew out a white puff of cold smoke.

Early that morning, she had felt his watchful eyes on her as she was getting dressed, putting on an extra sweater.

"We're going to be standing outside for some time, watching the women leave and I want to make sure I don't get too cold," she told him. He pursed his lips. If she was really honest with herself, she was angry at herself that she hadn't even brought it up once with Albert that she wanted to go on the march.

As she took the train up to the IRT station that morning, she wondered why she was even going. Even if Albert had permitted her to go on the march, how would she have been able to go away for two or even three weeks? She would have had to move mountains to ask Iris or other neighbors, whose lives were stretched themselves just to survive, to make meals, shop for their food on their limited budget, grab coal from the basement to their apartment and the list went on.

Helen then felt a hand on her shoulder. She turned around and saw Alice, General Jones and Harriot standing behind her.

"Helen," Harriot yelled. The din of the more than 200 women gathered kept rising to a roar that made passersby stop and stare at the unusual spectacle.

"Yes," afraid to say more that they would hear her discontent.

"You should be going on this March," Harriot continued.

"Yes, you should, dearie!" General yelled, her usual tone, not one just to be heard over the roar. "This," waving her arms excitedly "wouldn't have happened without you."

"Thank you, Helen," Alice said, putting her hand on her arm. This meant more to her than the others. "As soon as we are back, we are planning the March at Wilson's inauguration. You have to be there." Helen finally let her eyes well up and the tears flowed.

CHAPTER 17

Window New Life

HELEN KNEW IRIS WOULD be walking home a little after 5pm when the Factory job got out. She left her suffragist office a little early and headed towards her old factory, which was now out of her way, to meet up with her.

"Helen, what are you doing here?" Iris said, wrapping her coat tighter around her.

"Just wanted to say hello," Helen answered, putting out her hands palms up. She walked over to Iris and linked her arm through hers. "Tell me, how has it been at the Factory? How's Frank these days?" Iris glanced sideways at her.

"Frank is the same. The factory is, well, paying me every week." They walked a block in silence, arms linked tight to combat the wind. Finally, Iris asked, "How's your job?"

"Oh Iris! I was so involved in getting a big group of women to march from NYC to Albany. I helped find homes for the women to stay in. These women came back tired but with more energy—hard to believe!" Helen wanted to continue but felt Iris' attention wane. But she added, "What really upset me, though, was when I saw the women leave from the IRT platform, I was so angry that I wasn't with them."

"Why were you angry? Did Albert say you could go?" Iris asked.

"But that's the point! I didn't even ask him. I just knew he'd say 'no.'"

"Well, did you try?" Iris asked.

"Nah, it never seemed like the right time. He's talking about Abigail so much."

"You don't want to talk about Abigail?"

"Of course, I do Iris! It's just that I'm also," Helen paused for a moment "joyful at my job." Iris stayed silent. They walked for a few more blocks together in silence. Helen couldn't tell if Iris was angry or just didn't understand her. They were almost home and Helen asked,

"We have a rally next Saturday to follow up. Do you think you can join me? Please Iris?" Iris just shook her head.

"Frank would never let me. He even said, 'Don't get involved in the Helen Fox nonsense.' Besides Helen, who'll mind the babies?"

"I see. The older ones help out some," Helen said bending her head down but squeezed Iris's forearm. They reached the steps of their building and saw two neighbors standing in front talking. The ladies looked up, shaking their heads and Helen immediately felt wary. The news of her job had spread like wildfire through their insular community.

They started their attack: "Ya think your too good for us now Helen?"

"Must be nice not working in a factory."

"What'cha going to do with all that extra money?"

Before Helen even had a chance to respond, Iris called out, "Shut yur mouths you bats," and pulled Helen up the stairs through the front door. Inside the foyer, she turned to Helen and said, "It's bad enough the boys don't get it, we dames gotta stick together."

Helen was speechless. Iris was still her friend. She didn't need those batty women.

CHAPTER 18

Albert's Permission. 1913

HELEN LEFT WORK in a hurry, wanting to get home as soon as possible and also get out of the office. She had barely been able to focus that day. It was January 1913 and the suffragists were organizing an elaborate parade to coincide with President Wilson's inauguration in March. As Alice Paul kept saying, no one had staged an event of this magnitude, especially at a Presidential inauguration. Helen was skeptical if she could go: she had to get Albert's permission and besides who would pay for it? After the recent march to Albany that she hadn't been able to attend, she had felt especially isolated in the office. The exchanges revolved around the women's bonding narratives of the cold and the successful march. The chasm between her and the other women felt increasingly wider: savory meal descriptions, domestic staff anecdotes and weekend homes were all conversations she couldn't contribute to. Some of the women, like Alice, were unmarried but many others had spouses that seemed to unequivocally support their autonomy. She didn't have either. How was she going to manage the deliberations and be expected to facilitate the upcoming parade plans but not attend? She just needed to talk to Albert.

She felt a pit in her stomach walking home. She quickly stopped at the carts on Mulberry Street to pick up a few items for supper, vegetables and loaf of bread. A clam purveyor caught her eye and she stopped for a moment. Men were standing around the cart sucking down the raw, briny membrane oysters, almost passionately. Was their ravenous frenzy just imbibing sustenance or perhaps a teaser of a better life? The purveyor couldn't open them fast enough with the knife in his hand. The growing pile of discarded shells on the side signified the popularity of this cart. The vinegar and other sauce bottles were flying in the air as the men splashed them to accentuate their gastro experience. Albert could've easily been one of these men; he was fond of oysters so she had tried them once but hadn't wanted to again. She needed to connect with him; sit down and talk with him; convince him of the parade. It wasn't going to be easy, especially with the children underfoot in a small cold apartment.

"Your clothes lookin' clean," the building housekeeper Gladys said as Helen approached her building, holding the netted bag. Helen tried to walk around the rug Gladys was beating clean with a broom.

Helen coughed from the dust in her face and answered, "I suppose they are. I'm not at the factory anymore."

"Oh yeah. I heard. Where are you now?"

"With the suffragists."

"What's that?" Gladys asked putting her broom down.

"It's a group working on getting women the right to vote," Helen answered, one foot on the step closer to the door.

"Why would we want that?" Gladys looked at her, shaking her head, dust flying in a swirl above both their heads.

~

"Mama, when will supper be ready? I'm hungry!" Eleanor whined. Helen had walked in later than planned and found Walter and Claudia preparing the potatoes. She quickly started frying ground pork on the stove. When should she talk to Albert? During supper? After the children were asleep? A horn honk from down on the street snapped her back to the sizzling browned meat in the pan.

"Mama, did you like the potatoes I made? You didn't eat a bite!" Walter asked during their meal. Helen was looking out the window into the darkness. Leftover scents of charred meat and earthy boiled potatoes lingered in the air.

"Hmmm, good," Helen muttered.

"Yea—except for the lumps," smirked Claudia.

"Not at the table," Albert growled. "Tasty dinner, Helen. Meat twice this week? Oh, yah, we have extra coins from your job now."

"Did'ya go to work at the ... what're they called ...?" Claudia asked.

"Suffragists," she pronounced it slowly. "I did. We're planning a big Parade when the new President comes to office." She didn't mention that it was in Washington D.C.

"What's so special about a parade?"

"Everyone sings songs, chants sayings about something they believe in. Plus, there will be bigger crowds—we hope—for the new President."

She looked at Walter but he wouldn't make eye contact. She leaned over and ruffled his hair but he pulled away. He seemed to withdraw when she shared about her new job. Helen wanted to keep talking about parade plans. She *was* excited even amidst her conflicted feelings of exclusion. But she paused for now; this was all her family could handle.

"Tell me Claudia, what did you learn today?" Claudia started jabbering on about the *Secret Garden* book and the hopscotch game she and her friends played in the courtyard at recess.

"I'm going to meet James at the Whitehall tavern for a pint or two," Albert declared as they were cleaning up after supper.

James lived down the hall. Helen walked up to him, gave him a peck on the cheek and asked, "I'll wait up for you?" Albert shrugged.

Later that evening, Albert stumbled into the apartment. Helen had stayed up to wait for him, determined to ask his permission to go: no more procrastination. He took his shoes off, and they accidentally hit the wall.

"Albert! Shhh, the children are sleeping."

"The boys were really talking tonight." Helen could smell the alcohol on his breath. She sat up, took a deep breath and pulled her long braid from the back of her neck to the front of her chest and stroked it.

"They demanded I pay for the rounds," he said. Helen raised her eyebrows.

"Because my wife makes more money than me!" he said.

"Oh Albert. I just want the extra money to help us. Especially since we don't have Abigail's money." The words hung in the air. "I hate that those men are saying horrid things to you." She stood up, walked over to him, took his hand and guided him to the couch to sit next to her. She rubbed his shoulders, his back and felt him loosen up under her.

"We have to talk."

"More news? The ladies at your office tired of you?" Albert said.

She took a deep breath; this was not the time to defend herself. She needed his permission.

"The suffragists asked me to join them in Washington. They need help for the parade."

"They need an extra maid?" Albert muttered. She didn't respond.

"You need me to let you go."

Helen nodded.

"So what happens when those rich ladies are done wit ya? Will they dump ya like yesterday's garbage?" Helen bit the inside of her cheek. The thought had crossed her mind as well.

"Albert, please let me go," she said softly.

"Who's gonna cook? Shop for food? Mind the littles?"

"Claudia could tend to Eleanor and Walter could shop for food. I'll talk to Iris. Mrs. Miller from upstairs, she can look in on you." She paused, then said, "I can give a few coins to Susan, Gladys's daughter, to help." She regretted the words as soon as they escaped her mouth.

"Oh, now you're so rich you have extra coins to pay others?"

"Albert, it's not like that. Please ... I really, really want to go." Her voice remained soft. She leaned over and put her hand on his arm. "It's good for our family."

"Helen, I'm no fool—it's good for you. Only you."

She rubbed his neck and massaged his head. He softened under her fingertips.

Albert leaned over and kissed her firmly on the mouth. For a moment, she didn't respond and then kissed him back. He tugged at her braid pulling her closer and she leaned her body into him. They moved to their bed on the couch as their kisses grew more heated, their tongues deeper. Both moaning with arousal: innumerable months of pent-up estrangement came to the surface. He rose from the couch, shrugged his pants off and lifted her nightgown. She arched her back inviting him, even taking his hands and guiding them to travel all over her body, areas he had never explored. She could feel his anger dissipating. He entered her, his pants around his ankles, and they moved together in silent unison, their bodies joining until they both felt their bursts of desire.

Afterwards, they both lay on the couch, barely touching, breathing heavily. He stood to shrug pants back off and she shifted her nightclothes down to cover herself. He got back into their bed.

"Albert, Albert," she whispered.

"What is it Helen?"

"Sometimes I feel that working with the suffragists can ... right the wrong of what happened to Abigail."

"Nothing will bring Abigail back."

"I know. I know. I beat myself up every day for letting our sweet angel go work in that factory. I will never forgive myself until the day that I go rest in a grave." Albert still didn't say anything and she thought he had fallen asleep. While she was impetuous, he always took his time to process and respond over time. She would bring it up again tomorrow, at least she had asked him.

As she was falling asleep herself, he replied, "You can go, Helen. Go to Washington."

CHAPTER 19
Gentleman's Farm

HELEN WALKED INTO the suffragist's office, took off her coat and sat at Harriot Stanton Blatch's rolltop desk. Harriot hadn't been in the office as much lately and insisted she sit there. Helen wondered when they would give her, her own desk. She took her sweater off; the office was much warmer than her apartment. Harriot walked up to her, surprising Helen.

"Harriot, wonderful to see you. How are you feeling? Sit, sit," Helen said, standing up so Harriot could take her chair. She dragged another one over for herself.

"It's good to be out of bed. I couldn't stay supine any longer. I'm sure my children will give me grief for coming here but I had to see how the parade planning was faring. Only two months away!"

"I've really missed you," Helen leaned forward.

"Me too, my dear. My aches are taking over these days but this parade is carrying me to better spirits. Has Albert given his permission for you to come to Washington?"

"He has," she said, blushing, thinking of the previous night.

"That's great news," Harriot said, clapping her hands.

"I'm still surprised. I didn't think he would. Traveling to Washington—leaving my family—we don't do that."

"Most women, especially from your neighborhood, don't

83

leave their family. It's true. Mabel's husband won't let her go—we were disappointed. But it is happening more frequently now. We need you at that parade, Helen! Alice has told me how much you've been helping her."

"She has?" Helen pressed her lips together.

"What is it?"

"I don't know—she doesn't tell me much," Helen said.

Harriot then crossed her arms. "Don't take her indifference to heart. Alice was raised a reserved Quaker girl and she's not one to straightaway accept someone into her inner circle. But we're fortunate to have her and I'm thankful for her perseverance. She'll come around, don't worry."

"Quaker?" Helen asked. Harriot let out a big deep laugh causing Helen to redden.

"Aahhh, the Quakers: betterment of society. You'll meet more of them—we have more Quakers here than I would have thought. Alice *is* a conundrum. She was raised on a gentleman's farm in New Jersey, taking part in farm chores but also had a telephone and tennis court," Harriot chuckled.

What kind of farm has a tennis court? Helen thought. "Time to get back to the parade," she said.

"I'm delighted to catch up with you, dear. I'll be here tomorrow. Just need to keep convincing my children that I'm healthy enough!" Harriot exclaimed and moved to the couch in the main room.

Walking to the revolving bookshelf along the wall, Helen looked for the atlas with maps of Washington D.C. streets. Alice Paul had given her instructions on how to research routes for marching in the parade.

"Come Helen, let me show you the atlas over here," Lucy Burns had come up to her at the time and showed her how to read it. Helen stood taller and embraced the learning opportunity, grateful for Lucy's inconspicuous guidance. Helen had only met Lucy a handful of times; she was a close friend of

Alice's; they had met as suffragists in London at a police station.

As if on cue, the front door swung open, and Alice walked inside mid-conversation with Lucy and another woman Helen didn't know. Lucy smiled over at Helen. "I just don't understand why they can't write a bigger check. Don't they see how much their money makes a difference? We need to pay for our staff and more!"

"Alice, not everyone is as devoted to the cause as you," Lucy responded. It was true: Alice lived, ate, slept and breathed the suffragist movement.

"That's not fair, Lucy. Don't they see how we are helping them as women? I'm tired of hearing their well-intentioned refusals. I am going to keep asking and asking and asking until they have no choice but to open their pocketbooks and support the cause." Alice looked up and saw Helen.

"Helen, hello. Crystal, have you met Helen Fox?" Crystal shook her head, crinkling her eyes. "Helen is our star recruit. She's very valuable." Helen beamed.

"Have you been able to enlist volunteers from your neighborhood?" Alice asked. Helen's face fell, thinking of Gladys from her building and the neighborhood women's comments.

"I'm still working on it. I'm nearly done with the routes for the parade," she answered.

"Grand," Alice turned to Crystal and Lucy and said, "How many floats do we have now? Have we scheduled their order yet?" She didn't wait for them to respond and continued, "Ladies, ladies. We have so much to do. No one has staged an event of this size, especially at a Presidential inauguration. Only two short months away!"

CHAPTER 20

Last Minute Parade Prep

THE PARADE PLANNING was in full frenzied preparation mode. Helen walked into the New York office just days before the first bus was set to leave.

"Helen! Helen! The programs you worked on came in," Lucy Burns said, pointing to a box near the front door. Helen hadn't even taken her hat and coat off and picked one up.

"Alice was right, the cover looks brighter and the detail adds so much," Helen said. She and Alice had worked on the program together. The cover's title read: "Official Program Women Suffrage Procession" with an illustration of a knight in a shining armor announcing "Votes for Women." The Capitol building loomed in the distance and in the forefront were bright blooming yellow trees, which swirled into optimistic yellow clouds signaling a great happening about to occur. Flanking the knight were six women dressed in white with shiny purple satin sashes waving ribbons, ready to march.

"We've got to hit the sidewalks. Even though the parade is in Washington, we need to let New Yorkers learn about the parade and join us to march. Hand these out. Here's a list of corners to canvas and a list of volunteers to coordinate." Helen threw the program back into the box, pleased she hadn't even taken off her hat and coat. Behind Lucy stood a group of women, all with their hats and coats on holding stacks of flyers. They looked to her as their leader.

"Ladies, follow me. Let's go to Madison Avenue first," She had been studying street corners in New York as well as Washington and felt energized by Lucy's and Alice's vote of confidence.

They were soon on a busy street corner in Midtown, watching pedestrians pass by carrying shopping bags, running errands and on their way to work. Helen whispered to her group of volunteers, "Ladies: target local women but let's also soften the attitudes of the men," repeating phrases she'd heard Alice say in the office. Anne Baxter, standing to Helen's right started shouting at the crowd.

"Ladies, do you believe in the importance of women voting?" A few stylish women in thick wool winter coats, buttoned up to keep the blistering wind out, holding boxes from a nearby department store stopped and nodded their heads. "Then show your support by joining us for the Suffrage parade on March 3rd in our nation's capital down Pennsylvania Avenue." The shoppers clutched their purchases closer to their bodies and hurriedly moved on.

Before Helen could say another word, the volunteers joined the loud chanting and shouting. Anne Baxter was chanting so loud, the feathers on her hat waved about wildly, nearly falling out. Crystal Eastman, thrust flyers in any person's hand walking by, even though her coat, which was almost a long cape in thick camel hair wool with two holes for her arms, barely let her move about.

"Ladies, are you tired of being excluded?" shouted Anne. To their surprise a few women stopped. "We're marching in protest of our present government which excludes women. Join us for the Suffrage march on March 3rd down in Washington." Some took the flyers but many wouldn't make eye contact and quickly walked away.

As the day wore on, the negative responses deflated their morale:

"I'll have to check with my husband."

"I've never marched in a parade."

"Will I be arrested?"

"The newspapers here haven't responded to us and don't want to cover the parade," Helen said to Crystal, who was standing next to her.

"If the Tribune said yes, the others would follow: The Sun, The Evening World—heck even the racing papers," Crystal said counting them off on her fingers.

"Now, little miss, why would I want to come out in the cold and see a group of women marching?" a man behind Helen guffawed. She smelled the sharp smell of his cigar.

"Sir, do you believe in equal rights for all men?" she challenged.

"Well, yes," he hesitated, leaning over her with his bowler hat. She did not cower.

"Why not women then?" she pressed.

"Well ... women and men just have different needs and roles. That's the way it is," he said, stroking his white handlebar mustache, twirling it on the end.

"Yes, that's the way it is but that's not the way us women want it to be. We want equality and starting with the right to vote," Helen said, straightening her stance and looking him directly in the eyes.

"My wife doesn't feel that way," he said, no longer amused.

"Have you asked her if she feels that way? Sir, I just ask you to come to our parade next month and please bring your wife. When you see the outpouring of women *and* men marching for voting rights for women, we hope you will change your mind."

"I'll see about that. Good day," and off he walked. Helen felt the pats on her back of encouragement.

"We are out of flyers. Great job, ladies. Let's rest up for a different corner tomorrow."

"Helen, don't you think they will just throw the flyers in their fireplaces?"

"Well ... hopefully they will read them quickly beforehand."

She walked home, her feet swollen but her heart filled with assurance.

CHAPTER 21

Packing

HELEN KNEW SHE WOULDN'T be on the first bus carrying suffragists from New York to Washington D.C. leaving February 1st. That was reserved for the biggest donors and higher profile women.

"Alice, is there room on the second bus? I have to finish working on the floats in Washington," Helen had asked days before, also pointing out that she was in charge of booking the buses.

"Yes. We'll definitely get you a spot," Alice answered. While the parade date wasn't until March 3, 1913, they needed ample travel time and a head start on groundwork preparations to orchestrate all the moving parts. Helen vacillated between frenetic anticipation that the departure date would never arrive to angst about how she would actually leave her family. Would they survive without her? Would she survive without them?

"I've just heard from some women we've been courting: Mrs. Lew Bridges and Mrs. Russell McLennan. Their husbands will be in town for the inauguration and they thought it would be a swell idea to join them and attend our parade the day before," Lucy Burns said.

"I suppose they will wear their furs," Alice said. Helen furrowed her brows but envied the warmth of the fur, knowing she'd never have the chance to ever wear one.

While Helen wasn't going to be on the first bus, she still went to see the women off. Standing on the corner of Madison and 34th Street, she held up her hand to block the low hanging winter sun. Women were tightly squeezed together, elbow-to-elbow, standing on the top of the open-aired, poorly constructed platform bus, all waving flags jubilantly. It was a windy day, making the banners on the front and side of the bus flap. This only intensified the energetic buzz in the air, prompting bystanders to stop and draw further attention. The banner on the front of the bus, hanging from the second level, simply stated: "Votes For Women" with stars all around the words. Another banner, right behind the driver and covering the entire side of the second level said "National Women Suffrage Association," and listed details about upcoming rallies.

The driver stood on the curb, looking bored and not in a rush to finish his cigarette. He ignored the eager glances from the women, impatient to start their considerable journey and smoked his cigarette down to the stub. Finally, he threw it on the ground, crushed it out with this foot and said, "All right dames, where to?"

After seeing the bus depart, voices hoarse from cheering, the remaining women went back to the office. Helen found Harriot and General Jones deep in conversation and sat down with them.

"Helen, Helen, I'm thrilled you'll be part of the next procession venturing to Washington," General Jones bellowed. Helen smiled, rubbing her hands together.

"Is there any chance you can come?" Helen asked Harriot. Harriot shook her head, "I wish, my dear. I'm just not able to handle the physical travel. I'll be there with you in spirit! My job is to ensure the New York papers stay abreast of the parade," Helen gave her a fake smile to mask her disappointment. Harriot was still her only authentic champion. She never felt completely comfortable that the other women accepted her role.

She tapped her fingers on her armchair and asked General Jones, "Where will we stay on our travels and in Washington?" yet wanting to say, "I can't pay for my room!"

General Jones tipped her head back and laughed. "We've got it cobbled together. We're staying with Nicole Gorman in Philadelphia for a night and then we've arranged rooms at the homes of suffragists in Washington."

"Thank you so much, General," Helen said, holding back tears of relief, feeling a huge weight lift off her shoulders.

"We need to make sure we save a few rooms for the women walking to Washington," Harriot added.

"Walking?" Helen asked, putting her hand over her mouth.

"Yes. These women are determined to prove their commitment. We've arranged homes for them to stay along the way with provisions to keep them fed," General Jones answered.

Why would women walk when they can get a bus ride? I can't imagine having that dedication. Helen thought, tilting her head.

"Their dedication is admirable. I've got to make sure the newspapers hear about this!" Harriot said, as if reading Helen's mind.

~

Once Helen knew her travel plans for Washington D.C. and the suffragist parade were set, she rushed home to set forth preparations for her absence. Was she really traveling to Washington alone, leaving her family? Was she really going outside New York state for the first time in her life? Between the travel down and back and the actual parade, she would be gone for a few weeks. She walked into the apartment intending to pack and make arrangements.

The apartment was unusually quiet: Albert was lying on

the sofa, his eyes shut and the children were playing outside. She still couldn't believe that he had allowed her to leave for the Parade in Washington, even if begrudgingly so. She couldn't share with him how scared she was of traveling alone. She quietly walked into the bedroom, grabbed a small bag and set out a change of clothes: one outfit with another to spare and an extra sweater. Tiptoeing to the kitchen cupboard, she took a few cans and root vegetables that would last. She had so much to do she ignored how scared she was. She went back to the bedroom; Albert walked in behind her and sat on the bed, watching her make plans for a life outside their world. He cleared his throat.

"There are extra coins in the can," referring to the can nailed in the closet that held their savings. Tears sprung to her eyes.

"Are you sure? We'll need them to pay Gladys's daughter for watching Eleanor when the older children are in school. Remember she used to help us when I worked at the factory? Plus extra coal for the stove," Helen asked. Albert nodded and Helen added, "She can also help prepare meals."

"Nah, Claudia and Walter will step up. I'll make sure."

"I'll remind her but let Claudia know to use up the canned beans and preserved peaches from last summer."

"Won't we need those for the rest of winter? When you're back?"

"We'll make do. I want to make sure you're all taken care of while I'm ... away." She sat down on the bed next to him and started rubbing the back of his neck, massaging his head. He purred like a kitten.

"Albert. I know you know but I can't say it enough—it means the world to me that you are letting me go. I know it wasn't an easy decision."

"No, it wasn't. None of the other men I know would let their wives go."

"You're right. They wouldn't."

"Can we just say you're going to visit your Mama—she's taken ill?"

Helen just shook her head. "I promise not to brag about it."

"Does Iris know?"

"She does, but I need her help. She'll be looking in on you and the children. She's not a gossip, though."

Albert took a deep sigh then looked at Helen directly. "Just please come home. I've lost Abigail, I can't lose you, too."

Helen hugged him tight and said into his chest, "I'm not going anywhere Albert."

The next morning, early before the sun rose, she debated if she should wake up the children to say goodbye. They had said their farewells the night before. She decided just to kiss them gently on their foreheads. But the children woke and suddenly Eleanor was holding onto her legs not letting go and crying into her skirt, "Don't go Mama, don't go Mama." Claudia reassured her little sister, holding back her own tears, muttering she'd do her best to be in charge and Walter mumbled a few incomprehensible words, barely nodding his head. Making eye contact with Albert, all she received was a forced smile. Still she looked at him and the others and said, "I love you. Thank you. God bless." Albert mouthed, "I love you." Helen closed the door behind her.

CHAPTER 22

Bus Trip to Washington

HELEN'S BUS WAS FLAGGED by yellow automobiles on each side, adorned with Suffrage banners and signs advertising the upcoming parade. Slushy snow covered the streets along their journey, but it didn't stop local supporters from shouting well wishes. Her courage was like the snow. It started and stopped, waning in and out. Her life felt uprooted again. Did she rush into taking this trip? Had she forgotten to show Claudia where the extra canned peaches were? Why did she press extra coins into Walter's hands and not Claudia's? Would Albert forget to look after Eleanor? She was still so young at six years old and needed extra hugs, especially since Abigail was gone.

She took a seat on the bus next to Elisabeth Freeman, a volunteer, and they barely said a word to each other for the next hours. She sat as close to the window as possible, not wanting to have any part of her body touch her fellow passenger. She wanted to speak to her, but her mouth and throat were frozen with a rock manifested in her gut. She hadn't realized how difficult it would feel leaving her family, yet it combined with the eagerness to be part of this suffragist parade.

"First time on a bus?" Elisabeth asked her as they were eating rolls with butter and ham handed out by another volunteers.

"How did you know?" Helen asked.

"You haven't stopped staring out the window."

"Is it that obvious?" Elisabeth nodded.

"Everything is moving so fast. We are going through the towns at a dizzying pace," Helen said. "I've never left my family," she added.

"We'll be in Washington before you know it," Elisabeth said. Then also added, "Your family will be waiting for you when you come back. Do you have any daughters?"

"Yes. Two," not able to say she used to have three daughters.

"Then you are creating a better world for them!" Elisabeth said, making steady eye contact.

Helen swore she saw two children racing alongside the bus reminding her of Abigail and Walter when they would run around the neighborhood: a reminder of her oldest daughter's unnecessary death, which only affirmed this mammoth undertaking. Her first daring act had been getting on the bus.

It was dark when they reached Miss Gorman's stately Philadelphia Brownstone to spend the night; just being in a different state was a maiden experience. Even with the late hour, a crowd of women greeted them, with a few unsavory men offering unwelcome solicitations.

"Shouldn't you be drinking afternoon tea now?"

"You're more use on the farm to help me with my cows." The women let their banners and signs, "Votes for Women," answer for them, remaining silent. Helen watched as the signs waved higher and the men retreated, a dance in the women's favor.

"Where are your skirts?" one last call came from the crowd. Elisabeth Freeman held her sign steady, "Women. Use Your Vote," above her head in a confident manner that put the men at bay.

Ushered into the red brick building with a white stately

doorway and blue shutters, Helen felt enveloped into safety. The building was nestled among a row of brownstones on Walnut Street, creating a solid footing to rely on. Walking through the narrow hallway, her boots clicked on the polished wood floor and up the mahogany stairs as she was led to a luxurious bedroom. She went to sleep alone in her own bed for the first time in her life, looking at the embers in the fireplace with a full belly and an exhausted body. Her breath calmed to a normal pace for the first time that day, confirming her conviction and building her courage to continue her travel.

The next morning at breakfast, Helen inhaled the steam off a bowl of hot oatmeal placed before her, wide-eyed that someone was even serving her. The earthy smell unlocked her heart; Washington D.C. now seemed closer and New York City farther behind.

Boarding the bus, Helen took her seat beside Elisabeth, looked at her and did a double take. She had been so overwhelmed the day before: getting on a bus for the first time, wondering if Eleanor would recognize her after being gone for weeks, wondering if there would be any coins left in the can to keep them warm during winter. Was she sending the wrong message to the older children, Walter and Claudia, by leaving? Her life had been uprooted to fight the fight.

Elisabeth was dressed like a gypsy: gingham scarf tied around her head, long open overcoat with a shirt with billowy sleeves, vest with hanging tassels and brightly pleated peasant skirt with a sash of different colors tied around her waist.

Helen asked in a fast, short-winded voice, "Good morning, Mrs. Freeman. What are those?" motioning to the stacks of pamphlets in Elisabeth's hands.

"Please call me Elisabeth. I've got a mandate to sell this suffragist literature for my publisher. It's how I'm paying my way." Helen nodded, awestruck that formalities could melt away so instantly.

Over the next few hours, Helen and Elisabeth Freeman didn't stop talking. They were both from similar poor backgrounds and in no time were swapping stories of their paths to becoming suffragists.

"I was living in London and my life was incredibly tedious. My mother and I were making silk ribbon flowers for nobility. One day I saw a woman being beat up by a burly policeman and went to help her. We both ended up arrested and only when I was in jail did I find out why—she worked with the suffragists! At my first parade, I had a spiritual awakening looking down the line of the marching women. Their faces were turned to heaven, their expressions uplifted me," Elisabeth shared.

"My first parade was with my daughters. The ladies were dressed in white like angels also coming from heaven. They smiled at the hecklers, quieting them with their divine presence," Helen spoke the words out loud for the first time.

"And how did you become a suffragist?"

Could she share about Abigail? It was still so raw.

"My daughter Abigail died in the Triangle Shirtwaist Factory fire. I met Harriot Stanton Blatch at the fire. She was a ... a savior." The two women were finally silent, the weight of their personal commitments and newfound connection seeped in. They spent the rest of the bus ride in silence, Elisabeth holding Helen's hand. With a soft sigh, her breath now steady, Helen closed her eyes, feet ground to the bus floor, feeling rooted in her seat. She was ready to tackle the unknown of what awaited her in Washington.

CHAPTER 23
Washington

THE BUS DROVE OVER the bridge connecting Maryland to Washington D.C. late in the afternoon, the winter sun low in the sky. Helen could barely see the city through her tears, the large majestic buildings in the distance were blurry and looming as she stared at them in disbelief. Was it a mirage? To calm herself down, she kept repeating in her head: *Claudia, Eleanor, and Walter will never work in a factory like Abigail. Never. I'll make sure of that.* Her chest tightened, feeling a pang of panic as the bus pulled up to the NAWSA Suffragist Washington office. The address, 1420 F Street, NW, was familiar from looking at the Washington atlas repeatedly.

Helen opened the door and walked into the office, looking down at her sullied gloves and quickly taking them off. Alice Paul greeted the women right away.

"Welcome to Washington! You made it! We have so much work to do!" Alice's own hair was falling out of place and her dress was wrinkled. Helen sat in a nearby chair, overwhelmed. What did she expect? That Alice would come over and put her hand on her shoulder, rub her back and ask her, *Helen, how was your first bus trip?*

"Flyers to hand out, floats to finish, skits to arrange, so much work!" Alice continued, raising her fingers to tick off items. The other women who had arrived with Helen fluttered around and got to work. Helen didn't move. Why was she so bothered? She put her face in her hands to catch her breath. She felt a hand on her shoulder.

"Helen, Helen. Are you well?" she heard Alice ask. Helen lifted her head and saw Alice handing her a handkerchief. She sat frozen.

"Please," motioning for Helen to take it. "Take your time. We have plenty to do. Unwind for a moment and get used to the new surroundings."

Helen caught her breath and said, "I wish I could let Albert and the children know I arrived safely."

"We can send a telegram?" Alice suggested. Helen just shook her head.

"They'll be fine, Helen. Honestly. One day, our children will learn how much we need you here and how much you are helping them," Alice said softly. Helen wiped her nose with the handkerchief and kept nodding her head.

"I arranged for you to spend your time here at the home of Mrs. Althea Spencer in Georgetown. You'll eat a warm meal, get a bath, and get a good night's sleep." Althea was a widow who had inherited a great deal of money and generously supported the suffragist cause. She had opened up her home to volunteers from NAWSA in town for the march. The carriage outside the office whisked Helen to Althea's home. As the carriage pulled up to the house, Helen gasped. *How am I ever going to spend the night in this palace of a home?*

CHAPTER 24
Salon in DC

A BUTLER OPENED the door and greeted her: "Welcome, Mrs. ...."

"Mrs. Fox. Uh ... Mrs. Albert Fox?"

"Welcome, Mrs. Fox. We were expecting you," his voice neutral as he motioned her inside the foyer. She stepped inside the foyer, where she saw a large twinkling crystal chandelier hanging from the ceiling and in the middle of the room a gleaming mahogany round table with a large tall vase of arranged flowers. The moist scent assaulted her nostrils; she had never seen fresh flowers in the dead winter of February. The lights suddenly dimmed and behind the table a maid appeared, announcing, "Evening meal will be served shortly." Faint music and polite laughter came from a large room off to the side. The butler started to walk up the grand staircase and Helen just stood; he looked back at her and waved his hand for her to follow.

"We will show you to your room," he said. Helen took the steps slowly one foot in front of another. At the top of the grand staircase another uniformed maid waited, and without speaking, led Helen to a bedroom. On the bed lay a pressed skirt and shirt, clean shoes, and new undergarments. She looked Helen up and down and said, "The bathroom is in the bedroom, miss." *Was she joking? A bathroom right in the bedroom? Iris would never believe her.*

"The clothing is for you. Please feel free to leave your ... current outfit outside the door and we will launder it for you." Helen stifled a laugh. With a straight face she said, "Thank you, that'll be lovely."

"Dinner is served when you have ... freshened up." Helen had to stop herself from falling asleep in the bath and only pushed herself to get dressed because she was ravenous. The scent of meat cooking kept wafting up in into the bathroom. She sat down on the bed to catch her breath, feeling anxious, not used to being alone. The distraction of the bus ride and the anticipation of the Washington arrival hadn't given her much room to miss her children but she suddenly felt an intense longing. She wanted to remember exactly how shiny the chandelier was and the etched flowers on the furniture to tell the children; but how would they react when she narrated her lodging? Would they question what it had to do with the suffragist undertaking and getting women the right to vote?

What *was* she doing here?

"May I announce Mrs. Albert Fox," the butler said as Helen walked into the dining room. She scratched her new shirt and scanned the room for any familiar faces and, with relief, saw Crystal Eastman from the NAWSA office smile and raise her hand.

A short, plainly dressed women with a bun of gray hair came up and grabbed both her hands as she said, "Hello dear, I'm Mrs. Althea Spencer. Welcome to my home. I hope you find everything to your comfort. Please come join us for dinner." She pointed to an empty seat.

Helen sat and was served a plate of glistening food. She took small bites, afraid to throw up or overeat. She mimicked the women sitting next to her as to which utensils to use when the multiple courses were brought out. Even though the lights were dim, it felt bright in the room: charged energy and conversation brimmed with excitement about the upcoming parade.

"I hear there will be 3,000 people marching!"

"I heard at least 5,000." Women around the table oohed and ahhed, nodding their heads.

"Apparently Helen Keller will be giving a speech."

"She's been learning to speak and is much easier to understand."

After the meal was over, the crowd of women moved to the drawing room.

"Have you participated in many salons?" a woman asked Helen as they walked in together. She shook her head. A moment later, Crystal sidled up to her and whispered, "In our salons, we normally discuss politics and have readings by writers and poets. Tonight will be focused on the parade, of course."

"Thank you," she mouthed. *Did people really spend their free time doing such things? What a luxury it was to have free time and listen to poetry.* As she sat upright on a formal dining chair covered with a needlepoint cushion, she surveyed the room through Abigail's eyes. Would she have felt right at home in these unfamiliar surroundings? She never had the chance to figure it out. It would be different for her other children. Helen was tempted to grab the small cakes and put them in her bag to bring home to Eleanor: the child had a bottomless sweet tooth.

Althea Spencer started the evening off: "Ladies, this parade is the most visible and important demonstration that we as suffragists have ever attempted. We are all gathered here to take advantage of the lawmakers, the press and thousands of spectators in town for the inauguration."

Women quickly interrupted ....

"Well, we helped get Wilson elected and he better come through on his promise to pass the law for us."

"I'm not hopeful. I'm seen many of these politicians use us to help them and then cast us to the side when they didn't need us anymore."

"We need to use the influence of the Vanderbilts. I read that Alva has joined the campaign. Perhaps the politicians will listen to her moneyed voice."

"Why did this parade have to cost so much money? I heard Alice Paul raised nearly $7,000. We could be using those funds for events through all year." The actual number was closer to $14,000, but Helen didn't say anything. Alice had been fundraising non-stop and had said repeatedly, "We need the floats and pageants to be as beautiful as possible so the newspapers will cover us. We need to attract as much attention as possible."

"My husband and his friends don't support our cause because he said we'll vote for prohibition."

"Oh, that's hogwash! What does one have to do with the other?"

"Well, the taverns and breweries don't want to lose their business so they are petitioning against us suffragists. They're afraid we'll vote for temperance."

"Heaven forbid my husband loses his tavern to drink with the boys." A few women joined in nervous laughter. Helen laughed along and thought, *Would Albert vote like that if he couldn't drink?*

"Hear, hear"

"Hear, hear"

"Hear, hear." Helen could hear the gentle tapping of glasses raised in approval.

"My sister and I worked in the factories for years. The politicians need to hear our voices another way—through our votes. It's the only way!"

Helen whipped her head around to see who was speaking: a simply dressed woman whose face looked more weathered upon closer glance. Respectful clapping followed but no one responded. There were other women like her in the room!

"I do get weary always asking my husband for every cent and not having any money of my own," a well-heeled woman remarked. What she would trade for these problems though they did share financial dependency.

Helen's head swirled and she suddenly felt dizzy. The lack of sleep, exhausting bus-ride journey and now eating heavy food were too much to handle. Helen quietly slipped out of the room, wanting to take advantage of her own bed and room. She wanted to rest up and show her children and Albert that making the trip to Washington and the parade would make a difference in their lives, for the better.

CHAPTER 25

Parade Production

HELEN WOKE UP TO the scents of bacon grease, fresh bread, eggs frying and chicory coffee. Was she dreaming? She raised her arms over her head, feeling remarkably refreshed after just one night's rest encased in soft thick sheets in her own bed, a luxury in itself. As she got up to use the toilet in her room, the weighted guilt set in about her palatial settings. Her family would never believe she had spent the night here. How would she even tell them?

After breakfast, putting on her new hat and coat that had been on her bed the day before, she went to the NAWSA office in Washington, focusing on the parade tasks at hand. It was just days before the parade to be held on March 3, 1913.

Alice Paul called out to her as soon as she walked in the door:

"Helen, we need 100 children," Alice Paul paused for a moment. "Dressed in white."

100 children? Where am I going to find 100 children? Helen thought.

"It would be impactful if the children and women could strew rose petals around at the beginning of the parade."

Rose petals? In winter?

"The women should wear white robes. With colorful

scarves. They would walk up and present a tableau to stand for women struggling through the ages."

"Who will they present to?" Helen asked. *Where'm I going to find so many white robes?*

"Good question ..." Alice thought for a moment. "I know! Columbia! The female personification of the United States of America."

"Where will the women change?"

"Hmmm, hadn't thought of that." Helen felt a symbolic pat on her back.

"Live music should be playing to amplify the women marching. What about the triumphal march from Aida?" Lucy Burns interrupted. Alice nodded enthusiastically. "Trumpets, trumpets are impressive."

Aida? Trumpets? These plans are getting big, bigger ....

Alice didn't seem annoyed by her questions.

"Now, where will we hold the pageant?"

Finally! I know this one!

"Alice," Helen said, nearly shouting as she ran to get the atlas from the desk against the wall, "what about the Treasury building? It's right near Pennsylvania Avenue." Her atlas readings had paid off and she knew Washington D.C. much more intimately.

"Yes. Yes!" Helen realized she was good, in fact excellent, at handling the minutia details that buttressed Alice's vision of the parade; combined with Alice's connections of making it a reality they were a good team. She walked away to call a woman Alice knew about the robes and roses, awkwardly dialing the pedestal phone she'd only recently learned to use. She still couldn't quite fathom that in minutes the manual switchboard would spread news to other suffragists or allow her to speak with a volunteer in minutes, without a single letter, telegram or messenger sent. Most of the other volunteers, she'd learned, had telephones in their home.

"Oh, Helen, one more thing. We need a white dove to release at the end of the ceremony to signal the parade has begun."

White dove?!

~

A few hours later, Alice walked in excited, "Inez is in! She's agreed to lead the parade. I just got off the telephone with her. You know she's a lawyer," Alice exclaimed, "and she wasn't sure she should lead the parade. But she finally said yes."

"She's a lawyer? Women can be lawyers?" Helen asked.

"Oh, Helen," Alice paused and then laughed, "Do you think women can only be the domestic help?"

Ya, the ones I know. And work in the factories, she thought.

"Yes, she's a lawyer, in fact a very bright and accomplished one," Alice said.

"But also damn beautiful. It's just what we need for the parade and the men will love looking at her," Crystal Eastman added.

"She's a friend of yours?" Helen asked.

"I met her through my brother, Max. They had a tumultuous affair, years back, but are still friends. We became suffragists together." Helen felt her cheeks redden. Where she came from, they had another term for women who had "affairs."

CHAPTER 26

Parade

HELEN BREATHED OUT a puff of smoke and felt her eyes sting from the low temperature, yet she felt warm inside. She didn't want to pull her hat lower to shield her face in case she missed something. After months of working late on parade preparation, many missed meals with her family, gut-wrenching worry how she would travel to the parade and a momentous bus journey to Washington D.C., the parade was finally here: March 3, 1913. She didn't want to miss one precious second. It was a few minutes after 9:00am and she was standing at the Treasury Building waiting for it to start. She had been there for three hours already, ensuring everyone showed up, the floats were in place plus last-minute complications that arose.

Remembering the first suffragist parade she and Abigail had accidentally come upon, she stomped her feet to keep warm. How innocent and naive she seemed then, and how fearful. Watching the parade through Abigail's eyes: the unbridled enthusiasm, the youthful optimism. Everything had looked so new and unfamiliar. Now looking at the twenty-four floats lining up, the nine bands, four mounted brigades: it was personal with a sense of ownership. A group of women waved at Helen, the "Pioneers," who were in the first section to march: women who had been toiling for so many years for the suffragists. She had overhead their comments in the office applauding her involvement in the parade and the suffragist cause. They had even remarked how unusual it was to have a woman from the tenements working with them. Never complaining, completing every task on time and prepared for all their meetings, Helen overdelivered her duties, becoming nearly indispensable to Alice Paul and Lucy Burns.

Being unafraid to ask questions, taking charge of assignments and assuming responsibility before they even asked: Helen loved the person she had become. Yet she would go back in a second to the old Helen to get Abigail back. But how did she deny the happiness she felt, the exhilaration at seeing the possibility of women voting, especially at this moment? She even felt that her children were looking at her differently. Looking up to her more. Early that morning as she washed up, her face in the mirror looked different, younger than she had looked in years; forehead lines had disappeared, bags under her eyes had shrunk.

She didn't want to forget one detail when she went home and told Claudia, Walter, Eleanor, and yes, even Albert, about it all. Before she had left, she told Walter that the younger ones were his charge. How were they faring? Did they have hot meals at night? Was there enough coal to warm them when they slept? Was Albert home in the evening or drinking his way through the money in the can in the closet? Would they think she had changed too much in the time she was away?

"Helen, Helen, Inez is ready to go!" Alice called to her, bringing her back to the present. She watched in awe as Inez Milholland, as stunning as Crystal had described, dressed in a flowing white cape astride a striking white horse, named Gray Dawn, led the parade off to a start. How could one woman have the combination of beauty, intelligence and confidence so seamlessly, Helen wondered. The crowd couldn't take their eyes off her as her white cape flapped in the wind, with her crown displaying a large silver star shining in the sunlight, her long dark flowing behind her. A few drunken men catcalled but most were mesmerized by this vision in white.

"Helen, don't just stand there. Come in, quick," one of the "Pioneers yelled to her and motioned for her to join as they started marching.

I didn't come here to watch, she thought, raising her flag and adjusting her "Votes for Women" banner. And then she joined the women.

CHAPTER 27

Observations

HELEN'S CHEST TIGHTENED and she put her hand over her mouth. The crowd swelled in front of her and she felt panic rising. She had been marching for almost three hours. She moved her head away from wafts of tobacco floating by, the pungent smells of body odor, the drifts of horse manure. She had never been around a crowd this size with shouts, chants and marching footsteps: a rising hyper-state of tension.

"How many women d'ya think are here today?" Helen yelled out.

"I heard 5,000 showed up to march."

"Nah over 8,000."

"Who knew so many women would actually come?"

A harmony of voices:

"I know."

"Me, too."

"Yes."

"My thoughts exactly."

"Why are they dressed in costume?" Helen asked a woman marching next to her, shaking her head in disbelief. The group of women were wearing white coats, clothing she had worn when she worked on the farm as a child, and long black robes with square caps.

"Costumes?"

"They look like they're going to a costume party."

"The gowns are teacher's robes and graduates. The white coats are pharmacists and doctors. We're behind the working women coalition—women in the work force." Helen's eyes welled up. How stupid of her! But oh, those women were something.

Abigail could have become one of these ladies. If only she had finished school. She could've been one of these working ladies, bittersweet optimism laced with regret.

Horses hoofed, heels clacked, women chanted, policemen swung bats against their palms; each distinctive noise blended together, the din of the crowd rising. The noise pitch would go up, go down, and then rise to an even higher pitch.

"You look like the floozy I was with last night."

"Go back to the kitchen where you belong!"

"Look at those boneheads. They can march all the way to the North Pole but they'll never get the right to vote. Keep marching, ladies!"

"Go home. We don't want you here."

The men laughed loudly, booing the marchers. A group of policemen stood right next to them, poker faced with no expression. A minute later, without a muscle moving, Helen heard chuckling from under their mustaches, supporting the hecklers. These policemen were supposed to protect her, yet she felt particularly unsafe in their presence.

With the noise level especially loud, Helen noticed the faces of the women chanting, singing with their eyes closed, talking to fellow marchers, eyes shining with glee and optimism compared to the pursed lips of the policemen, with their eyes squinting in suspicion.

After a few hours of marching, her arms hurt and she kept trading flags with other women, alternating between the stars and stripes and one that said "Votes for Women" in large block, black letters. The flagpole stood over six feet tall and the flags whipped in the wind.

As the parade progressed closer to the Capital down Pennsylvania Avenue, the crowd was more jam-packed with spectators, with not an inch of free room. The mostly male crowd varied between men in top hats and morning coats to men with newsboy caps and working-class waistcoats. She barely saw a female face in the spectator crowd.

"How lucky are we that the inauguration is tomorrow!" a woman next to her remarked, visibly exhausted but still fueled by the forward motion of the parade.

"Why?"

"They've set up the stands for the crowd to watch and celebrate with the bunting. We're taking advantage of their preparation."

Ya, but these men would trample us in a second given the chance, she thought. She almost tripped over a woman lying down on the street in front of her.

"Ya all right, Miss?" reaching down to give her a hand to get up.

"Ya, those drunken fools tripped me and the policemen just stood there watching." Even though the woman wasn't hurt, Helen still seethed with anger.

The crowd of male spectators swelled as she marched on. The magnitude of the crowd seemed to get more bloated as did the size of the men. Or were her eyes playing tricks on her?

The pageant! she thought. She had almost forgotten, as she had been caught up in fear of the mostly male crowds.

I've gotta get there right away. I'm late! I can't miss it. I planned so much. She desperately wanted to reach the end of the procession but the amplified crowd had slowed down the pace of the parade. She left the parade route and took a detour to the Treasury building where the pageant was being held. She knew these surrounding streets by heart by studying the maps of

Washington when she was helping plan the parade back in New York. The streets were fairly empty as soon as she was off Pennsylvania Avenue. In just a few moments, she arrived at the Treasury building, with enough time to help Alice get the pageant off to a start.

CHAPTER 28

Pageant

HELEN HEARD THE FIRST few bars of the Star-Spangled Banner.

Alice's vision of the pageant is coming to life!

She then saw Columbia—she now knew who she was— dressed in a flowing robe of red, white and blue emerge from the columns at the top of the steps to the Treasury Building. The crowd watching gasped as she made her way down the stage and Helen couldn't stop smiling. She had helped put those smiles on the crowd's faces. The children scattered rose petals as women followed the rose-strewn path: Charity, Liberty Justice, Peace, and Hope—all in beautiful flowing white robes with colorful scarves.

"What's that tune?" a woman next to her asked.

"The 'Triumphal March' from 'Aida,'" Helen answered, grinning with her newfound expertise.

The children then ran up to Columbia and presented the symbolic tableau, written especially for the event. Afterwards a dove was released to signify the ending of the parade. Helen chuckled as she glimpsed the wings beating higher into the air. A dove!

How can we NOT get the vote passed? Helen thought, listening to the deafening cheers from the crowd. She looked around to congratulate Alice and spotted her standing with a man. Alice was gesturing strongly and delivering her message forcefully. Helen saw the man write on a notepad and nod along with Alice. That must be the reporter from the *New York Times* that Alice had mentioned, Helen thought. Right on cue he turned and she spotted his Press badge, in big black letters, pinned to the brown coat he was wearing. Stepping closer to them, she listened.

"This was one of the most impressively beautiful spectacles I've ever seen staged in this country," he said. Alice was beaming. Helen just hoped her friend would let herself enjoy the glory for a few minutes.

"Helen, Helen," Adele Draper, a volunteer from the New York office reached out from her fur stole to grip her arm, "Isn't this fantastic? Beyond our wildest dreams." Helen nodded with a huge smile.

"I heard from a friend of mine in government that President Wilson was watching the parade. He was shocked at how many women attended. Apparently, he's worried we will ruin his inauguration tomorrow," Adele said. Helen's jaw gaped.

"How could he think we'll ruin the inauguration?" she asked.

"He's afraid we'll turn Washington into a burlesque town with all the women attending. That's absolute malarkey!" Adele said laughing, stroking her fur coat. "He clearly has no idea the type of women he's dealing with!"

"Can he do anything to hurt us?"

"I did hear that he ordered extra policemen to patrol. I'm not worried. Look at how much the suffragists have done already," Adele said, waving her arm at the pageant and the crowd watching.

CHAPTER 29
Meelee

AS QUICKLY AS WIND changed directions, the parade was out of control. So many women had turned out to march that even after the pageant was over, they went back to marching in the streets.

Thank goodness the army is here. Helen thought. However, the relief was fleeting. Within moments, men charged into the street, no longer remaining the jeering spectators. Their actions declaring the parade over while mocking the suffragist cause. As they passed flasks to each other, their inebriation fired harsh comments like daggers.

"Hey lady. You look like the floozy I was with last night."

"That dirty crumb! How dare he say that to me?"

"Get your meathooks off me!"

"You Ladies will never get to vote. Not if I have any say in it."

"Dames are good for one thing and that's in the bedroom."

"Lady, if you are going to walk on the street, you should do it at night with the other street walkers."

"Did yar Mama raise you to act like a dog?" Helen screamed so loudly she didn't even recognize her own voice. Some men actually stopped in their tracks.

"You disgusting beasts," she yelled. The Helen from before Abigail's death, or even a year ago, would never have stood up to these men. However, it didn't quiet them down for long. Men trampled over women in the street. The female marchers tried to run away but had nowhere to go. The tone of the parade had shifted from orderly liveliness to utter chaos. When the policemen finally got involved, their horses became more of a hindrance. The street was so jam packed, marchers and spectators now intertwined, horses had no place to move. They acted up and inadvertently trampled people as well.

Helen gagged from the stench of rancid body odor mixed with alcohol emitting from the charging men. It reminded her of the odors of the animals on her childhood farm when they were in heat. Nobody was safe in their charging path.

She fell down while trying to run away from the crowd. While face down on the street, she heard horse's hooves but wasn't sure how close they were to her. The air was swirling with so much noise. Someone shouted at her: "Lady, move. LADY MOVE. That horse is about to trample you!" She lay on the street frozen. Her mind numbed her body and paralyzed it from action. Why couldn't she move? What seemed like an hour but really seconds later, an arm grabbed her up and away from the horse. She saw the hooves come down right where she had been lying on the street. She looked around to see who had helped her but didn't see anyone.

I'm not ready to die. The barrage of insults did not terrify her. Nor the slander of the suffragist movement. They even encouraged her fervor. What did terrify her was dying. She wasn't ready to die. She had too much to do. She had life inside her to love Albert and the children for a long time. Abigail's death was tragic and she was taken away from them way too young. She would only let her family down by dying. She also wasn't ready to give up working for the suffragist cause. She stood still for a few moments and gasped for air.

In the distance, Helen heard sirens of ambulances coming closer. She continued to hear them the rest of the day, coming and going. Women from all walks of life walked around with torn clothing, bloodied arms, mussed up hair, some carted into the ambulance. Casualties of hopefulness and ambitions gone awry.

While she ended up unscathed, many women were limping on the shoulders of others, helping each other. Women now locked arms to protect themselves from the increasingly vicious crowds. Drunk males had gone from onlookers to unsolicited participants.

The sirens started to die down and the crowd started to thin out. The men in military uniforms alongside the policemen eventually got the crowd under control. Helen surveyed the emptying street; it looked like a battleground. Papers strewn everywhere, trampled flattened hats, torn clothing, broken bottles and even a few bodies lay on the street. She smelled wood burning and saw smoke rising from a float. The wood-burning smell mixed with odors of burning clothing: an event that started joyous and notable gone astray. The fire department had just arrived to put out the fires. Seeing them nearly made Helen faint: a flashback to the fire of Abigail dying.

She then heard Alice Paul proclaim from a distance: "Thank you. Thank you. All of you who came today. We have invigorated our suffragist movement. We have given expression to the nation-wide demand for an amendment to the United States Constitution enfranchising women. You have given us hope that the future for women voting is possible." The cheering drowned out the rest of her words but it didn't matter. The parade was officially over.

Helen walked back to Althea Spencer's Georgetown home to collect her meager belongings. She was ready to go back home to Albert and her children. Her bus was leaving early in the morning. Holding her head up high, she wasn't the same person who had left a week before. If she had any apprehension of her dedication to the suffragist cause, that was gone now.

CHAPTER 30
Return to New York

HELEN WALKED ONTO the bus heading back to New York, saw the empty seat next to Elisabeth Freeman and sank her body down. Elisabeth immediately clutched her in a tight warm hug, allowing Helen to burst into tears, ensconced in the safety of her friend's embrace, her first secure moment since she left for Washington over a week ago.

"I was saving this seat for you. I was so moved, too. I still can't believe how many women showed up—from all over the country," Elisabeth said. Helen concurred.

"And the pageant! With Inez coming out on the white horse. Helen, your hard work really paid off," Elisabeth added, squeezing Helen's arm. She kept nodding but couldn't stop crying.

"You should be so proud of yourself! I overheard Alice telling Lucy that it wouldn't have happened without your help. What is it?" she asked handing her a handkerchief.

"I almost got killed!" Helen blurted out then proceeded to tell her the whole story how the horse had nearly trampled her in addition to the hostile policemen making her feel especially precarious.

"Oh yes, the policemen were particularly terrible, weren't they? I heard President Wilson sent them to keep us women at bay," Elisabeth said.

"I heard that, too," Helen agreed.

"But they can't keep us down, can they?" Elisabeth said. Helen shook her head still sobbing.

"Helen, is there something more?"

"How can I go back to Albert? What if he doesn't take me back this way?" Helen said between cries.

"What way? Did something happen?" Elisabeth asked.

"No, nothing else. It's just ... I know now I don't have a choice in being a suffragist. Seeing the thousands of women that showed up to the parade, how dedicated Alice, Lucy, all the women are and how terrible the men acted towards us. I don't have a choice. But what if he doesn't let me do this anymore?"

"He will Helen, he will. You've told me how loving he's been. Convince him this is for Abigail. For her memory. Make sure she didn't die for nothing," Elisabeth added, Helen wincing at her response.

"Yes. Yes. You're right. It's for Abigail," Helen said.

"Look what we've done, Helen," Elisabeth said pointing to herself, then to Helen, back and forth and waving her hand around all the women on the bus. Helen crinkled her nose and eyes, smiling through her tears. Elisabeth was her gift: she'd never had such unconditional love and support. They both soon fell asleep, exhausted from the parade, and eventually arrived back in New York.

Helen opened the door to her apartment cautiously, not wanting to wake anyone up. It was after midnight and she just wanted to crawl into bed and go back to sleep. She peeked into the bedroom, lightly kissed Claudia, Walter and Eleanor, sleeping intertwined in the one bed, her heart heavy with longing. Staring at their innocent sleeping faces, she had held in her worry that something was going to happen to them while she was gone. She started crying again, quieter this time; feeling a sense of relief that she had gotten home without harm and her children were taken care of. It was as if no one could take care of them except for her. But that wasn't true. They looked clean, well fed, in spotless night clothes and were safe and sound even though she had been gone for over a week. The first time a parent had left them in their short lives. Did they need her as much as she needed them?

She then crept into bed, careful not to disturb Albert. He automatically put his arms around her as he normally did when they slept. She assumed he was sleeping deeply.

"You're home. Thank goodness," he mumbled. He sprayed kisses all over her face, hugged her tighter, his eyes shut.

"I didn't want to wake you," Helen whispered, kissing him back.

"I barely slept while you were gone. I can rest easy now. We all missed you so much—the children and especially me," Albert said sleepily. Helen settled onto his shoulder hoping to fall back asleep.

"It's out of your system now?" he asked. Her eyes popped wide open.

"What do you mean?" she asked.

"Now that you're home and the parade is over, are you done with the suffragist rubbish?" he said.

"Albert, I'm confused. Where is this coming from?" she asked. He pulled a pamphlet from under their sofa bed. It was a picture of a man holding a crying baby with a pot burning on the stove behind him. The caption read, "Men—are you ready for a change of family life? Women are safest at home."

"Where did you get this?" Helen asked.

"Someone at my factory. They heard you were in Washington marching," Albert answered.

"Albert, do you believe this?" Helen asked, sitting up.

"Not really. But we did miss you. Claudia did all right with the cooking and Walter helped shop but Eleanor was always afoot and the older ones had a hard time watching her and doing their chores. Plus Claudia's cooking is terrible," he said.

"I can still cook and shop Albert. I promise you. Please don't make me give up my suffragist. It's part of me now. Plus it's for Abigail—her death ..." Helen pleaded. How could she give up now? She'd come too far.

"Well then, but promise me you won't leave again. It was horrid here without you, Helen."

"It sounds like you missed my cooking Albert, but did you miss me?" Helen asked.

"Of course, of course," he answered and wrapped his arms around her tighter. Helen wasn't convinced and tried to turn over and go to sleep but his arms wouldn't let her move.

PART 2

1916

CHAPTER 31
November 1916

HAD IT REALLY BEEN MORE than three years since the parade in Washington? It was still the most exhilarating event in Helen's life; even the bus rides to and from Washington and NYC, had been unforgettable. She had been afraid that coming home would be a letdown but the children had badgered her to share stories for weeks. She ignored the gnawing feeling in her gut that they'd survived without her and relished rehashing the parade events.

"Tell us about the pageant!" Eleanor demanded.

"Again?" Helen asked, winking at Albert.

"Yes! And we want to hear about the hundreds of children singing with the trumpets," Claudia added.

"There were only 100," Helen corrected, smiling.

"I want to hear about the fancy houses!" Walter said, more interested in her accommodations. She had been hesitant to describe the lodgings at first, but the children wouldn't relent.

"I still can't believe you had your own washroom, right in your own bedroom!" Walter said, shaking his head.

"Did 8,000 women really show up to the parade?" Albert asked, leaning forward.

"Yes, they did! As far as I could see, women were marching and cheering us on," Helen answered. She looked at him, straight in the eye, not blinking, comforted that his interest signified approval. Though he didn't ask her as much about the weekly rallies or marches she was involved with, he helped out with feeding the children or bringing coal and wood from the basement when she was late from work. His own union involvement had grinded to a halt: he had lost interest after Abigail died. She had asked him about it once when she got back from Washington and he shrugged his shoulders and said, "Not that important to me anymore." She didn't press him and was grateful that he was allowing her to stay involved with her suffragist activities. Her extra pay didn't hurt. He did go out more often to the local tavern to have a pint with the neighborhood boys but he didn't come home drunk and seemed content enough. However, he tickled her while she was making dinner and she would overdramatize how much his shoes smelled with the whole family ending in fits of laughter. Their playfulness caught them all by surprise.

Claudia and Walter seemed to have grown up nearly overnight. They took Eleanor to school, shopped for fruits and vegetables at the carts on Mulberry Street, prepared supper and kept the apartment tidy. At age nine, only three years younger than Abigail had been when she died, Eleanor no longer needed constant minding.

After the parade, the press had been nonstop for the suffragists. Helen, Alice, and others worked around the clock to capitalize on the momentum. Coffers overflowed and women beat down the door to volunteer. They all celebrated when Nevada and Montana states granted women the right to vote. Harriot's party, renamed the Women's Political Union, merged with Alice's party, Congressional Union, which was now called the National Woman's Party. The unification was much less confusing for Helen and allowed her to work with Harriot and Alice together. It was also particularly important given that the suffragist cause took a back seat to the war. Helen kept thinking that women needed to stop arguing amongst each other and work together which the unified party now did.

Unfortunately, President Wilson hadn't followed through on his promise to get a federal law passed; the Senate voted it down. There were other things to attend to—barely a year after the parade, war broke out in Europe. Albert's job at the factory was not affected by the war and they ignored Walter's pleas to enlist. He was too young.

Three years later, the suffragists were still waiting for the right to vote. Funds still rolled in—not as much as before, but they were still able to pay for workers including Helen's salary, thank goodness! And to plan publicity techniques, an annual convention and a large demonstration in New York City. Now with rumblings of the United States entering the war, the suffragist cause was taking a back seat to the war efforts.

It was barely 7am but Helen couldn't wait to get to work. The leaves were barely left on the trees and there was a hint of snowfall in the air. She loved this time of day, when the sidewalks and streets were still waking up, the morning's sidewalks washed clean from a storm the night before. Everything was shining: the jaunty store awnings, the morning light reflecting off buildings. It was worth waking up early for. She had prepared breakfast for her family in the dark; sliced bread, butter, jam and heated milk, tidied up the apartment and readied the stove by raking out the ashes and lighting a new fire.

"Why are you leaving for work early again, Mama?" Claudia asked in the darkness. Helen had hoped no one would wake up before she left.

"We have a few rallies next week I need to coordinate. I'll be home for supper, I promise!" she said, putting her hands into her skirt pockets. She thought they'd get used to her not being at home as much but it didn't seem to let up.

As she rounded the corner to the suffragist office, she

heard, "First woman elected to Congress, Jeannette Rankin of Montana. Git ya paper. Read all about it. Only 5 cents," hawked a newsboy on the street, waving a daily paper in his hands.

"Germans turned back in another battle. Allies move closer!" Another newsboy on an opposite corner yelled.

~

"Helen, we've got a few new volunteers today. Can you take them to the street corners uptown and get more signatures? For the rally next week? It's the biggest one in New York," Alice Paul asked her as soon as she walked into the office.

"Yes Alice, we don't want folks to forget about us. It's getting harder to compete with the war overseas," Helen answered. Even she found herself distracted by the headlines about the United States potentially entering the war. "I planned the rally next week, remember?"

"Of course, of course. Just so much to do. I know I can count on you, you've been here longer than most. It's just that ..." Alice paused.

"What?"

"I need to know you'll speak up if things aren't progressing, especially while I'm in Washington. I can count on you, right?" A sudden influx of women entered the office.

"Weren't you class of '09 at Swarthmore?"

"I was at Swarthmore, too! Class of '07. We didn't have any overlapping classes did we?" Viola piped in. She had become a new close friend of Helen's but they didn't discuss their education, or lack thereof.

"I miss working in the hospital, but I'll go back to nursing when the children are older and the vote gets passed," Lydia said. Helen looked down at her shoes for a moment.

"You can, Alice, I promise, you can count on me! We'll get hundreds of signatures," Helen said, turning back to Alice. She really meant it but heard the doubt creep into her voice. "You watch, this rally will be our biggest one yet!"

~

"Here you go!" Helen placed twenty-seven pages of signatures with at least thirty signatures and addresses on each page, on Alice's desk.

"I'm impressed," she said, smiling at Helen with her eyes and mouth; then she turned back to Crystal Eastman to say, "We need to set up more meetings with Representatives that are undecided. Oh Helen, can you finish the publicity campaigns we talked about?" Helen nodded.

"Alice, will Harriot be here today?" Helen asked.

"She hasn't come back from the meeting at the Coffee House with Lucy and some other women, Elizabeth Kent and Hazel MacKaye, I believe. Since our groups have merged, and it looks like Tammany Hall relaxed its opposition, Harriot believes that New York state will add a constitutional amendment to give us the vote!" Alice said.

"It's much less complicated for me now that Harriot's group has merged with the National Woman's Party. I was almost doing my job twice," Helen confirmed.

"That's correct! We are much more powerful as one group! With President Wilson's reelection coming up, we might actually get our Suffrage amendment introduced in the Senate," Alice explained.

"Will we endorse President Wilson?" Helen asked.

"Great question! We've been debating about that nonstop. At least with Wilson, we know what to expect. With Hughes, we have no idea where he stands," she said and turned back to her conversation. Helen walked away standing tall, her arms clasped behind her body. These conversations were now the norm. Helen's job in managing the organizers and volunteers in New York and other states were showing direct results. She walked over to a group of women sitting at the mahogany dining room table in the NAWSA office.

"We had the most delicious soup for dinner the other evening."

"What was it?"

"An onion soup simmered in cream sauce."

"How long did it take you to prepare?"

"Goodness—I didn't cook it! Belinda prepared it."

"Ladies, I need someone to help write the announcements for this week's ice hockey game," Helen interrupted again.

"A suffragist announcement at a hockey game?" one woman snickered.

"Absolutely! This is part of the publicity campaign for New York City. There's a suffragist vote coming up in New York State. We need to convince as many men as possible to vote for it. Even if we get a few boos, we'll get the men's interest." It had been her idea to promote the suffragists at sporting events. "There is so much to do and we don't have time for idle chitchat." The women quieted right away and Maude volunteered "Yes, Yes, I'll do it."

"Helen, I'm joining you at the Suffrage school tomorrow, correct?" Viola asked.

"Yes! I'll see you there first thing in the morning," Helen answered, excited about the prospect of spending the day with her new friend.

"Helen, can you read it over? Are we missing anything?" asked Maude, handing her the sports announcement. Even though Maude was a Columbia University graduate, she was also a recent hire, and Helen had written many of these over the years. "With the upcoming election, we do need to ask these men NOT to reelect officials opposed to the federal suffrage amendment." Helen read out loud.

"This is perfect. We have to stop being polite and start asking them to vote our way," Helen said crossing her arms

"Thank you, Helen," Maude said.

⁓

That night, she made it home before Albert and immediately turned to the stove.

"Eleanor, unwrap the lamb slices. Let's get the potatoes peeled." More often now, she was able to buy lamb slices already cut up and prepared from the butcher.

"Claudia, is the stove lit? I need water boiling!"

"Walter, we need more coal. Quick—dash to the basement."

Albert walked in, threw his hat and coat on the rack by the door. "Smells delicious. Been cooking for long?"

"No, Mama brought it from Mr. Driscoll," Eleanor informed. Albert looked at Helen and she held her breath.

"Great idea. Hard to cook lamb in a short time," Albert said, and Helen let out her breath. The can in the closet was finally filling up again; they had the money.

"Let me give you a hand," he offered, seeing Walter walk in with full arms of coal. "It's going to be cold tonight and we need to keep feeding the stove."

As they got into bed that evening, Helen nearly collapsed from the long day.

"I got another one of these at work," Albert said, handing her a pamphlet. It showed a man doing the laundry while his wife was dressed to leave the house. The caption read, "I want to work but my wife won't let me."

"Do you really believe this, Albert?" Helen asked.

"Nah. Supper's still on the table and I'm going to work. But the lads at the factory seemed to think they might get stuck at home doing the laundry," Albert said.

"Would that be so bad?" Helen asked laughing. Albert did not laugh back.

"Oh Albert. I'm just joshing. We don't expect you men to start doing the laundry. We just want the right to vote and protect our family. Don't you want that, too? Get rid of the cretins who couldn't protect Abigail?" Helen asked snuggling up to him, kissing his neck. He didn't smile but lay back, closed his eyes, allowed her kisses to flutter all over him and kissed her back.

CHAPTER 32
Pregnant

"HELEN, HELEN, did you hear me?" Viola asked.

"No, what'd you say?"

"Is everyone here and ready to perform the tableau today?" Helen, Viola, and other Suffrage volunteers were at an event held at a local school, driven indoors by the wet weather. "Let me check my list," she said looking at the piece of paper in her hand. She felt tired that morning, dispirited from not being able to do the event outside, where they had hoped to attract passersby.

"My first Suffrage school! Tell me again, what exactly goes on?" Viola asked.

"We hold skits based on famous suffragist events. They rehearse and then present at the end of the day."

"Why not just have an open-air meeting?" Viola asked.

"We want to attract women who aren't involved in politics. They don't necessarily have an interest in suffrage but are enticed by the theatre."

Helen cleared her throat. "Ladies, ladies. Welcome to the Suffrage School. We have divided you into ten groups, each of you doing one skit; here are your scripts. You'll rehearse and then present to the entire group at the end of the day. I recognize it's hard to shift our attention away from the war. We don't want to forget all our boys overseas," she instructed, hoping her voice didn't break and sounded more like these women. She'd been trying lately to speak similarly to the ladies in the office: not cutting off her words and using new vocabulary. Someone raised her hand and asked, "Was this written by a famous playwright?"

"No, not really. They are historical scenes," Helen answered.

"Historical scenes?"

"Yes."

Voila then interrupted, "There were performed by Helen Hayes and Marilyn Miller at the Ziegfeld theatre." The crowd of women oohed and aahed and then went on to begin their rehearsals.

One group recited "The Declaration of Sentiments" written by Elizabeth Cady Stanton at Seneca Falls, New York. Dorothy Myers was especially convincing, tearing when explaining that it was the first Women's Rights Convention. The women got engaged in the theatrics and the emotions of the female roles. It made Helen think about Harriot Stanton Blatch, Elizabeth's daughter, who had brought her into the suffragists right after Abigail died. Harriot was not around this office as much due to her in focus on backroom politics at Tammany Hall. She kept trying to convince the politicians that women would not vote for prohibition. No one had as much faith in her from the get go as Harriot had. Helen felt a pang of sadness but also wished Harriot could see her now: leading a group of women, planning rallies; how proud she would be.

A white woman, Ruth Goddard, was persuasive when she recited "Ain't I a Woman," a famous speech by Sojourner Truth, a former slave. Even Viola, who usually remained composed, dabbed her eyes.

One particular woman, Evelyn King, remarked that it was difficult for her to play Susan B. Anthony, because Susan had chosen not to marry. Evelyn and the other women in her group didn't agree with this which caused an uproar. They were completely missing the point that Susan B. Anthony didn't marry because she couldn't own property in her name. They did go on to show Susan B. Anthony casting her ballot for Ulysses S. Grant in the presidential election, then getting arrested and brought to trial.

Over the next few hours, the women became more and more engaged in performing, even reenacting the recent parade in Washington before President Wilson's inauguration. Mildred George acted as Victoria Woodhull when she addressed the House Judiciary Committee, arguing women's rights to vote under the fourteenth amendment. Her voice never rose but her tone was strong and definite.

As the women filed out of the school at the end of the day, they thanked Helen and Viola effusively.

"I haven't had this much excitement in ... I don't even know!" one said.

"Just tell your husbands to vote for the candidates on the list we gave you. We'll see you at the NAWSA office next week," Helen responded. A woman who had barely spoken a word all day pushed a wad of bills into Helen's hand as she walked out. She mouthed, "For the cause." Helen stood there, holding the stack, astonished.

"I'm exhausted but what a success! Three hundred new women attended. How many will turn into volunteers?" Viola said looking at the list of names on sheets of paper.

"Don't care," Helen shrugged. "Just want them to go home and tell their husbands about it. Don't need as many volunteers as we need their husbands to vote for better politicians!" Helen answered curtly.

"Helen, what's the matter?"

"Why?" Helen asked stepping back. No one ever asked her how she felt.

"I don't know. You seem ... distracted now."

Helen thought for a moment, feeling her achy legs, her lower back spasm and her tender breasts. Then she said, softly, "I'm late."

"What do you mean late? Oh oh oh oh! When did you last bleed?" Viola herself had four children.

"Not sure. Started to feel my lower back ache and realized I hadn't bled in months," she said quietly.

"Perhaps it's your time to stop bleeding," Viola offered.

"Good god woman, I'm only thirty-five. Four children, six pregnancies, I know my body and this can only mean one thing."

"Four children? I thought you had three," Viola asked. Many of her fellow suffragists didn't know about Abigail; though it was Helen's personal calling why getting the women the right to vote was so important, now wasn't the time to share about Abigail.

"I just can't be pregnant. The children are finally old enough that I don't have to keep them at my breast. What am I going to do?" She had always accepted her pregnancies, never even questioning if they should have another baby. "I have to keep working with the suffragists. It's given me purpose. A baby would just get in the way, keep me trapped at home," she whispered, suddenly regretting saying the words out loud. She waited for Viola to look at her with her hands over her mouth.

"You know, there are things you can do if you are pregnant," Viola said in a neutral voice.

"Things to do?" How did Viola know? She was married to a successful physician; a nanny raised her four children and they had a large summer house in Oyster Bay, Long Island.

"You don't have to keep the baby."

"I can't give my baby away!"

"No, no, no. You could have a 'miscarriage.'"

"A miscarriage?" Helen asked. She'd had two of them between pregnancies.

"A doctor would make it happen through surgery."

"A surgery would make me lose the baby?" Helen's eyes widened.

"It's a planned miscarriage."

"I don't know, I don't know. Does this really happen?"

"Helen. You aren't my first friend who's distressed about being pregnant." Helen was silent for a few minutes, listening to their heels clack on the sidewalk as they walked back to the office.

"Hmm...."

"There's an office downtown that helps pregnant women have a miscarriage. You must go as soon as possible, though. And please, please, please, I beg you, don't do anything at home to induce the miscarriage on your own."

Helen looked at her narrow eyed.

"Our children are blessings. I thank God every day for my four. But we are also women." Viola added.

"All my children are—were—blessings. But so is my work with the suffragists."

I'll wait a few more weeks to see if my bleeding comes and think about it then, she thought. Her body still felt fatigued but perhaps it was from the exhilaration of the ten successful Suffrage school events, rather than the pregnancy panic.

She ran into Iris in front of the building that evening on her way inside after work. Iris took one look at her face. "What's wrong, Helen?" she inquired.

"You know me so well!" Helen said, looking at Iris. Their friendship had only strengthened over the years. Iris never said one negative thing about Helen's involvement with the suffragists even though she admitted she didn't always understand Helen's unwavering devotion. Helen once overheard Iris scolding Mrs. Fitzpatrick, their nosy neighbor, in the hallway, "You don't know what you are talking about. Helen Fox is a great mother and wife. The suffragists haven't taken her away from her family at all!"

"I could tell the minute I saw your face," Iris said.

"Oh Iris! I don't know what I'm going to do!" Helen said.

"What is it? Albert lose his job? Are the children safe?" Iris asked.

"Yes, yes. They're all fine. I might be pregnant!" Helen blurted out. Iris's eyes widened.

"Oh Helen! Another mouth to feed?" Iris said. Helen sulked, her eyes welling up.

"Did you tell Albert?" Iris asked. Helen shook her head.

"What'll I do?" Helen asked.

"You'll do what we women have been doing for ages. We'll find that extra food, squeeze the baby into the bed. Plus, Claudia's old enough to tend to the baby, she can stay home from school. Even Eleanor can lend a hand. How old is she now, nine?" Iris replied. Helen took a deep breath and relaxed her shoulders. Her friend's support did comfort her but she didn't have the heart to share that her anxiety stemmed from the possibility of not working with the suffragists rather than the burden of the additional child.

CHAPTER 33

Birth Control

A FEW WEEKS after the Suffrage School event, Helen bumped into Viola outside the Suffragist NAWSA office building: Helen coming from downtown and Viola uptown. Viola started to remove the pin from her hat with her thin lace gloves.

"I assume you aren't pregnant," Viola whispered, looking at Helen's flat stomach.

"No—thank goodness! I started bleeding again. So relieved!" She didn't add that she pushed Albert away every time he wanted to have sex. She was afraid he'd start looking elsewhere if she kept refusing him. She had never even told him she thought she was pregnant. As soon as she started bleeding, she ran to Iris's apartment; they both jumped up and down, hugging and laughing in relief.

"Helen, there is something you can do to prevent this scare, how to not get pregnant." Helen looked at her with a furrowed brow. Viola started laughing which made Helen's cheeks redden.

"This is a fun problem to help you with. I know exactly how to help. We have to fulfill our marital obligations. You can use a condom. Actually, Albert uses it."

Has this woman gone mad? Helen thought.

"What are you talking about?"

"A condom goes over his member before ... " Viola shared expertly, her hands starting to gesticulate. Helen could barely look at her.

"Oh gosh, I don't know ...."

"You want to make sure his liquid doesn't go inside you. The condom helps with that."

Looking at Viola, Helen put her hand over her mouth.

"My husband and I use them all the time," she said, putting her hand on Helen's arm. If even possible, Helen's cheeks turned even more scarlet.

"Viola, what if someone hears you—us—talking? Could we get arrested?"

Viola started laughing again. "Dear, it's perfectly legal. Besides, everyone is rushing to get somewhere, they're not minding us one bit." She waved to a woman striding by, shopping packages in hand, dragging children behind her, and another man in a suit on his way to work.

Could this work? Could I still fulfill Albert's desires and ... my desires and not get pregnant?

"Does it fit?"

"Yes, it does. My husband claims he doesn't even feel it anymore and he's a physician! There are different materials: linen, goat intestines," Viola said while Helen listened, resting her chin on her hand.

Helen wondered how Albert felt at that moment about having more children. He had once shared that it would be respectable to have another child to replace Abigail. Helen answered in shock, "No one and nothing can replace Abigail," and they had never discussed it again.

"Where do you get them?" Helen asked.

"By mail or there is an office downtown that sells them." Viola paused for a second, "I have extras. I'll bring it in for you tomorrow."

With that Viola opened the door to the office and held it

for Helen, "After you. Let's get our day started."

True to her word, Viola brought in a few for Helen the next day. She even showed her how to use it on a few fingers as Helen watched, speechless.

That night, as Albert was whistling after the evening meal, Helen decided to introduce her new discovery. She was actually looking forward to having sex with him without the worry of getting pregnant. After the children were asleep in the bedroom, they undressed, headed to the sofa and she cleared her throat, "Albert, how do you feel about having more children?"

"Do you have something to tell me?" his face panic stricken.

"No, no, nothing like that. I'm not pregnant." His face showed immediate relief.

It had seemed so easy when Viola was showing her but now she wasn't sure she'd have the nerve to introduce this strange object going over his penis.

"There's something we can do to not have another baby but still be together." He smiled.

She had been holding the condom behind her back and took it out. "You put this on. Over your ..." and pointed at his penis.

"Where in hell's name did you get that?"

"It's so ... we ... I don't get pregnant," she said, her voice shaking.

"Helen Fox. There is no way in hell I am putting that thing on."

"Well, Albert Fox, I can't have another baby! We can barely afford to feed and clothe the ones we have now. Besides, a new baby will never replace Abigail," Helen said.

"How does it work?" he asked, after a few long minutes. Helen delicately showed him, thankful that her path to freedom was paved with these new condoms.

CHAPTER 34

April 1917. War

"HEY ALBERT, did you hear about Henry?" Fred asked.

"Nah." Albert kept his head down, staring at his whiskey glass. He was sitting at the bar in McSorley's tavern.

"He enlisted!"

"Enlisted?" Albert looked up.

"Bloke, don't you read the rags?"

"Heck I do!"

"We're at war with the Germans! Wilson declared last week. Haven't you heard?"

"Of course, I've heard," he said through clenched teeth. It was all anyone talked about.

"Well, he did it! He's leaving for basic training in a few days and then shipping overseas," Fred shouted.

"What about his job? His family?"

"His family? They're over the moon! He's a soldier in uniform now. I tell ya ... remember when the Germans sunk that boat? What was it called?" He paused, then tried again, "Ummm— the ... the ... Lusitania. Gee, I hated those Germans. But I didn't want us to go to war." Fred downed the rest of his drink in one big sip. "But now, I'm ready. I'm going down to the recruitment office and enlisting. The old lady isn't going to be too happy about it. See ya later pal."

"Sam ..." Albert nodded at the bartender pointing to his empty whiskey glass, not ready to go home yet. After Abigail's death, he had given up fighting the unions at his factory. He now felt that personal void, especially compared to Helen who was fulfilled with her suffragist purpose.

Walking home that night, the recruitment posters popped out at him: on buildings, wooden fences, and in store windows next to mannequins with tailored men's suits. He found himself transfixed in front of one, staring at a large finger pointing at him, "I Want You" it read. Albert felt like Uncle Sam was talking directly to him.

A few weeks later, Albert walked through the door and bent down to take off his dusty boots, only the floor was crowded with boxes of suffragist pamphlets; they lined the wall by the front door in their already cramped apartment.

"Oh, sorry Albert. Those boxes will be gone by this weekend; we have a big rally on Saturday. Claudia, this is the one you're coming to," Helen called out from the kitchen as she doled out Shepherd's pie.

"I'm tellin ya, Joseph said his Pa got a whole new set of clothes," Walter said, his arms waving in the air and his voice raising decibels higher.

"New clothes? Wow," Eleanor said, her eyes widening.

"He did not," Claudia said. "I'm sure he got a new uniform and undershirts, but he did not get a completely new wardrobe." Claudia, at age fourteen, was a voracious reader with her nose always in a book, causing her to act like the final authority whenever there was a dispute. Walter ignored her.

"He said he'd never seen buttons so shiny, shoes so bright and everything brand new—no hand-me-downs. He's going on a trip to Europe in a big ship 'cross the ocean!" All three children, even sixteen-year-old Walter, stood there with their mouths agape.

"He's not going on a pleasure trip. You do know that children, don't you?" Helen said.

"Papa, Papa! Joseph's pa joined the army. He's fightin for our country, in a new shiny uniform." Albert looked down at his soiled clothing and dirt-darkened hands.

"I'm not happy about President Wilson declaring war," Helen said.

"What do you mean, Mama?" Eleanor asked.

"I don't trust him. I'll never forget the boatload of promises he delivered to us suffragists when he was elected in 1913. The stars, the moon, the right to vote. What has he done? Nothing! We still don't have the right to vote and he's even put some of our women in jail. He's only getting us farther from the cause. I'm not a fan!" she said, her hands on her hips. Albert crossed his arms.

"Helen, I'll not have you speak ill of our President in this house. It's unpatriotic. We must support our President and our country at this time," Albert said. Everyone at the kitchen table looked up at him.

"I'm not unpatriotic, I'm just saying …."

"Our country's at war and we gotta support our soldiers. Put your suffragist views aside. Focus on our men. They need us."

"Why can't we have both? Why can't women have the right to vote and men go to war? Why are we forgetting about our rights? I just don't think President Wilson is going to do anything for us women. He's never going to give us the right to vote while we are at war," she said, biting her bottom lip.

"Enough!" Albert yelled, slamming his fist on the kitchen table. The waning light in the apartment made him look much older than his 39 years.

CHAPTER 35

Enlisting

ALBERT WALKED RIGHT BY the ivy-covered building on Duane Street near City Hall. He froze when he saw the long line snaked around the corner. The sun's rays warmed his face and the temperate spring air quelled his nerves. A woman pushing a baby carriage smiled at him as he heard cheerful conversation around: spring had arrived and city dwellers were thawing out after another harsh and hibernating winter.

"Chap, this the line for recruitment?" Albert asked a teenage boy at the end of the line. He looked Walter's age, sixteen or seventeen, and was wearing a newsboy cap slung uneven off the side of his head, a tie, vest and proper suit jacket and pants. The whole outfit looked borrowed and combined with his close-shaven face with a few inexperienced nicks around the neck and collar, he emanated uneasy assurance sprinkled with a dash of doubt.

"Yes, sir. Ya joining up, old man?" Albert knew he looked fifteen to twenty years older than most men on the line. Most didn't even look eighteen: the minimum age to enlist. He had dried himself out, not drinking one drop of alcohol for nine days straight, and even took an unpaid day off from work resting on a co-worker's couch—without Helen knowing, of course. He wanted to appear as bright and well-rested as possible. He smelled the stringent shoe polish wafting up from his feet, having polished his shoes that morning for the first time in months.

"Yup, I'm joining up. Don't be such a wisenheimer, I'm not that old." He surveyed the other men in line and smelled the body odor. They were all here of their own free will but it didn't diminish the trepidation working against their initial rash decision to enlist. He felt the sweat run down his back and tried to ignore it.

I need this, he thought.

As the line slowly progressed, Albert saw a sign that read "Orderly Room" with an insignia of the U.S. Army tucked underneath. In front of the door, stood two men in uniform. One was smooth-shaven and the other wore a mustache, both dressed in khaki green wool uniforms. Their jackets fell below their waist with a slit cut up a few inches on each side. Shiny gold buttons lined all the way to their neck met at the buttoned collar. The jackets had two breast pockets with a pleat and one man wore a leather strap across his chest, under the lapel and then traveling down to tuck into the leather belt around his waist. Their uncuffed pants had a sharp pleat crisply ironed down the front.

The one with the mustache started the questions.

"Name?"

"Albert M. Fox."

"Age?"

"Twenty-nine," the man looked up at him for a split second and then wrote it down. Albert almost let out a sigh of relief.

"Address?"

"117 Hester Street, New York City."

"Married?"

"Yes," Albert had agonized how to answer that question.

"Children?

"Yes."

"How many?" Another question he had agonized over. Too many was a deterrent.

"One."

"Any injuries or disabilities?"

"No sir. Healthy as a horse!"

"Go on in for the physical." The mustached officer waved him inside the building into darkness: an unknown destination. Albert put a hand up to shield from the bright sun while he peered inside. He couldn't see anything and walked into the darkness. His eyes still hadn't adjusted so he followed the voices. He arrived at a closed door, opened it and walked in on a medical exam in progress.

"Hey man! Wait your turn!" shouted a naked man sitting on an examination table and a man in a white coat listening to his chest. He quickly shut the door and waited outside.

A few minutes later, the man in the white coat opened the door while the now dressed man scurried out. "Come in. Name?"

"Albert M. Fox."

"Please take off your clothing," he said without looking at him while writing on a clipboard; he then motioned towards the examination table, which looked as if it hadn't been cleaned in weeks. Was the man in the white coat going to leave while he undressed? He didn't move so Albert started taking off his clothing very slowly, piece by piece.

"I don't have all day. Hurry it up. There are a lot of men out there." Albert was soon naked. The man in the white coat started by listening to his chest.

"Take a deep breath." He proceeded to give Albert a full examination: peering down his throat, looking up his nose, listening to his heartbeat, measuring his spinal posture, feet arch, knee reflex, balancing on one foot at a time, handling his rectal and testicular. He listened to his lungs a few more times.

"How old are you?"

"Twenty-nine, Doc."

"Are you working?"

"Yes, Sir."

"Where?"

"Mercantile Factory."

"Uh-hmmmm," the man in the white coat said as he wrote on his clipboard. Albert tried to look at the clipboard but couldn't see what he was writing.

"All done here. Get dressed and wait in the room down the hall," the man said. Albert put his hand on his chest to calm his beating heart, afraid the man in the white coat would hear.

He got dressed and walked with leaden feet through the dimly lit hallway to the waiting room. There were men seated in rigid wooden chairs and benches, no one making eye contact, each knowing that one of them could be instantly denied entry to the army. A soldier would enter, call a name and a man waiting would stand and follow him to another room down the hall. No one was saying one word. Albert watched as each of the men, even men who had come in after him, were called until he was the last one waiting in the empty room. He had to keep stopping himself from drumming his fingers too loud on his pants for fear of the soldiers directing him to keep it quiet.

"Albert Fox. Albert M. Fox," called a different soldier.

"Yup, here," Albert said, stood up from the rigid wooden bench in the waiting room, tripped over his feet and nearly fell flat on his face before he caught himself and then stood straight.

"Follow me," the soldier said, and took him into a room with soldiers sitting at a desk with papers in front of them.

"Mr. Fox. I'm sorry but we have to deny you entry to the U.S. Army. You did not pass the physical examination," one of the men said and lifted a stamp to cast down on the paper.

None of the men in the room made eye contact with Albert. "What're ya talking about? I'm healthy as a horse! Been working every day of my life," Albert said, louder than he would have liked.

"I apologize, but you failed the physical and we can't take any chances," another man answered.

"What part did I fail?" no one answered.

"Ya gotta tell me what I failed," his voice wavering.

"The Doc said your lungs don't sound good. You been working in the coal mines?" the soldier said, almost laughing. Albert thought about the dust and chemicals he had inhaled for the last twenty years in the factories.

"Nah," he mumbled, slung his cap back on his head and walked out as fast as his feet could take him, his head hung low.

He started walking aimlessly. All he saw were men walking on the street in uniform. He hadn't told Helen or the children that he was enlisting. If he had, he'd imagined how the conversation could have gone.

"Albert that's the most insane idea I've ever heard. What are you going to do over in Germany? You're not a soldier."

"Helen I gotta fight. Support our country. Like you're fighting with the suffragists."

"I'm not fighting, Albert. We're just demanding for the right that is due to us as people, as women. The right to vote." She'd worked so long with the suffragists; she knew all their arguments by heart.

He had also played another moment in his head, when he would walk into the apartment through the front door in his new shiny uniform.

"Papa! You look so handsome," Eleanor would cry out.

"Yowzers—can't wait to tell Joe my Pa's enlisted, too!" Walter would pat his back.

"Oh, Albert. I can't say I'm happy about you enlisting. But

now that you have, I'm so proud of you. You're serving your country. And that uniform fits you so well," Helen would say, throw her arms around him, hug him tight and plant a big kiss on his cheek.

~

"Hey simp, watch where you're going," he bumped into a man on the sidewalk walking towards him. He looked up and the sun hit him right in the eye. It was still sunny outside, but a dark cloud hung over him with rays of sun piercing through the clouds, burning his skin and his eyes.

"Excuse me," Albert mumbled. He found a new tavern on the next block and walked in.

CHAPTER 36
Drying Up

"ALBERT. ALBERT."

"Hmmmm"

"Albert, get up."

"What? What do you want?"

"You smell like an outhouse." He tried opening his eyes but they were crusted over. He could only see a shadow of Helen.

"Where am I?"

"Get up! Change your clothes, wash your face, take a bath. Do something. Ya stinking up the apartment and we need to air out the place," Helen said. She nudged his shoulder with her foot.

He rolled off the sofa onto the floor and caught a whiff of his own body odor, gagging. He then smelled something cooking. Meat? Was it breakfast or supper? The windows were grimed and streaked with soot so provided no clue as to the time of day. He looked down at his body and gasped at how filthy his clothing was: dark creases of dirt and excrement; he quickly bowed his head.

"Papa, you finally awake?" Eleanor asked him.

"Have to get dressed. Go to work," Albert mumbled.

"Not till the morning," Walter said. "It's 7 o'clock at night."

So that was supper, he thought, not able to look at Walter. He sat up and a wave of nausea swept over him while at the same time his stomach grumbled from hunger.

When did I last eat? he asked himself.

The last thing he remembered was walking into the tavern after leaving the enlistment office but couldn't remember when that was. He wanted to ask what day it was but was too embarrassed. He felt his cheeks burn with shame at the U.S. Army rejection. He would never tell Helen or the children about his enlistment attempt. He didn't want to see the look of pity in their eyes. The way they were watching him now only confirmed this thought.

"Claudia, can you help me? Your handwriting's so much better than mine. I need to gather all these different sheets of papers with names onto one list and count how many names we got," Helen asked and sat down at the table, ignoring him.

"What are all the names, Mama?" Claudia asked.

"Remember that street corner we went to last week and collected all those signatures?" Helen asked. Claudia nodded.

"We've gone to several others and have lots more."

"Are they all for the ... what's it called?"

"A petition. That's right, we need to collect 1,000 names, put our heading on it and send it to President Wilson. We're almost there! Even though we're at war, we need to keep sending him as many petitions as we can so he doesn't forget about us suffragists."

Albert watched Helen and Claudia sitting at the table, their heads bent towards each other, engrossed in counting names and diligently writing President Wilson. Claudia, at age 14, was already a young woman emulating her mother. His heart sank and chest tightened when Helen mentioned the war, the army enlistment scene flooding his memory. He wished it was just a bad dream but instead felt the disgrace of the aftermath.

"Look at you!" Helen cried out. They all turned around and

saw Eleanor twirling around with a white ribbon that read "Votes for Women" over one shoulder and waving a flag that read "Let Women Vote."

"Get that off. Ya too young," Albert muttered, barely audible.

Later that evening, after all the children had settled themselves to sleep in the bedroom, Albert had eventually risen off the couch and cleaned himself off in the hallway bathroom. There wasn't any more hot water, yet he still waited in line for a cold bath. There was a newspaper lying on the floor in the hallway; he picked it up and glanced at the date. He had lost three days! No wonder Helen had looked at him with such contempt! The cold-water bath had been worth it and had revived him. As he walked back into the apartment, shaking his wet hair to dry off, Helen looked at him from the kitchen table.

"Albert, come sit. I've made you hot tea and toast." She had opened wide the windows to air the apartment. While it was chilled in the air, the offensive smell had disappeared. "You need to eat something," she said gently. The thought of food still made him nauseous.

"I'll take the tea," and positioned his face over the steam coming from the mug. The tea leaves opened his nasal passages, and he could smell the alcohol coming out of his pores.

"What happened?" Helen asked. He flinched slightly but didn't answer.

"We can't go on like this," Helen continued. "Ya haven't worked in days, maybe more. I've got my paycheck from the suffragists but it's not enough. We need your weekly pay. You know we can't survive without it."

After a few moments of uncomfortable silence, she coughed and said, "It's more than that, Albert. This isn't the man I married, the man I had children with. The children need you as a father. I need you as my husband."

Albert looked away because he didn't want her to see his

eyes welling up. He felt a lump in his throat. He wanted to pour out his heart and tell her everything that had happened.

How he had felt so old standing in the enlistment line.

How he woke up one day and felt that he had wasted his entire adult life toiling away in the factory. He wanted those years back.

How he missed Abigail so god-damn much and thought about her every day.

How he felt dried up inside and sometimes drank to moisten that arid emptiness.

How he knew he was letting her down. Letting the children down. Walter was nearly his age when he had gotten married! He couldn't even look him in the eye.

He didn't say anything but finally looked at her, his eyes wet. She put her hand over his and he really looked at her. It was the end of a typical long day and her bun had come slightly undone. Tendrils of hair had fallen out and framed her face. It softened her appearance and gave him courage to speak.

"I don't even know ... I don't even know ... where ...."

"Well you can't quit your job."

"I know, Helen. I'm not quitting my job."

"Albert, please come closer to me," she put her hand on his arm. "Please. I'm sorry. I'm just ... I'm just ...."

"What?"

"I'm just scared. I can't lose you. When I—we— lost Abigail, I thought the world was going to end. But it didn't. I feel like I'm losing you. We're losing you," she motioned towards the bedroom, her voice wavering.

"I know it doesn't always seem that way, but we really need you around here. The children need their father. I need a hus-band. I love you," she didn't move but she also didn't take her hand off his arm. He felt the heat radiate throughout his limb. It felt good. The nausea finally started to dissipate.

"Is there any more of that meat pie? A little grease would probably be good for my empty stomach." She nodded and stood. "Let me warm you a piece." While she had her back to him, he felt the courage to speak more. His mouth salivating at the scent of the store-bought meat pie heating on the stove.

"I need more," Albert said.

"What do you mean?" Helen asked, turned around, her face in a grimace.

"Like what you've got with the suffragists. To be part of something. To be needed and appreciated."

"We need you and appreciate you."

"Nah. Not that same. You should know that, too. Look how rewarded the suffragists make you feel."

"Well, you could help us out. Now with the war, we suffragists really have to struggle to get people's attention. Coming from a man is especially helpful."

"Nah. That's your cause. Not mine." He wanted to tell her that he had tried to join the army and fight for their country, but that it hadn't worked out. Helen stood up to turn down the light. He mumbled quietly, "I'll figure it out. Let me quickly eat and then let's go to bed. I have to get up early tomorrow for work."

CHAPTER 37
Walter Enlists

Walter walked through the doorway into school, P.S. 184, and turned a sharp left to hide inside the doorframe. He then took a few deep breaths, waiting to make sure his mother had left. Sometimes she'd join Eleanor in her walk to school and she would continue on, to drop off Walter at the high school, leaning in to kiss his cheek. Normally, he pulled back but he let her today. He saw her turn the corner on her way to the suffragist office, her white sash swaying behind her. Did she have to wear it all the time? She disappeared from his view and then he headed back out into the street in the opposite direction.

The school bell rang and immediately the scene in front of the building changed, all the school children rushing inside. Walter looked up at the building and then towards the street. The sidewalk was now filled with women holding net bags on the way to the market, dragging toddlers behind them; one little boy stopped to pull up his knee socks. Walter looked for his father in the sea of men on their way to their factories, holding their lunch pails with their heads down.

That's not how I want to end up, he thought. He wrinkled his nose, smelling roasted nuts from a cart next to trash thrown out in the street. He crossed the street to escape to busy Delancey Street with signs promoting "Laundry," "Tailor," commingled with flower merchants peddling their daisies and tulips.

Even at this early hour, the busy street was clogged with cars spewing their dark smoke and choking noise. Walter didn't mind as he stopped to admire the various models out on the street: Roadsters, Model Ts, Tourings and even a Coupe. He dreamt of learning to drive and owning a car; wearing a fancy chauffeur uniform or even maneuvering the streetcar pulling on its track. He ran a few more blocks and bumped into Raymond.

"Where ya been?" Raymond barked.

"Whadda ya mean?"

"It's already 8:30!"

"I told you I'd come when my old lady left me at school," Walter said, catching his breath. "Do you have another smoke?" Raymond handed him a cigarette from his jacket pocket.

"Ya better enjoy it. We won't smoke these for a while. Let's hit the road!"

Walter and Raymond started walking fast but soon their nerves slowed them down. Soon they ended up at the enlistment office on Chambers Street. Walter didn't want to admit how scared he was: of his parents' anger but also the unknown of what lay behind the enlistment office door. Had he thought this through enough?

"Do you have another smoke?"

"Nah, we finished the pack."

"What? Already?"

"Don't forget to tell them you're eighteen," Raymond reminded.

"Ya right," he said impatiently.

"Ya know you're not old enough?" Raymond had said.

"Hey, I'm almost seventeen."

"Ya gotta be eighteen for the army."

"You're not eighteen!"

"Almost. They're gonna see that baby face," Raymond teased, squeezing Walter's cheeks. "Just lie and say you're 18. They'll believe you."

The line moved quickly. Walter kept looking around at the other boys in line.

"Do you think they'll give us our rifles today? I can't wait to shoot those stinkin' Germans!" a young man said in front of them.

"Don't be such an idiot. You first have to go to basic training," a man in front chided. Before he knew it, Walter was in front of the line, talking to two soldiers. He had no way of knowing that they were the same soldiers his father had spoken to just a few short weeks before.

"Name?"

"Walter Fox."

"Age?"

"Eighteen," the man didn't even look up.

"Address?"

"117 Hester Street, New York City."

"Married?"

"No."

"Children?"

"No."

"Injured?"

"No."

Walter passed the physical with flying colors, a strapping seventeen-year-old who hadn't had to work in the factories like his father and sister, and even his mother, before she worked for the suffragists.

"Did that creep touch your balls?" Raymond asked him as they walked out of the enlistment office in their shiny new army uniforms.

"Yeah, you, too?" Walter nodded, looking down at his shoes. They both laughed nervously, fingering the buttons on their jackets, stroking the wool khaki cloth of their new uniforms, nervously adjusting the too big hats and walking awkwardly in shoes that didn't fit.

Walter noticed the looks he was getting on the street, especially from women. Old women, young girls, teens, mothers pushing baby strollers looked him up and down and smiled.

"Did you see that dame? She batted her eyelashes and licked her lips at you," Raymond goaded.

"She did not, you fool," Walter blushed from the unaccustomed attention even though he loved the looks. "I need to kill a few hours. No one's home yet."

"My sorry old man ain't been home in weeks and my mama's working late at the Nelson family. What'll your folks say when you walk in wearing your uniform?"

Walter sighed, "My Mama will probably cry ... I might be knocking on your door for a place to sleep."

CHAPTER 38

Walter in Uniform

"WHOA. You better go right into the bedroom before Mama sees you," Claudia said as soon as Walter walked into the apartment. Eleanor stopped stirring the pot of stew on the stove, ran right over and hugged him hard.

A moment later, he heard the crash.

"Please tell me that uniform is a prank," Helen cried out, her hands on her apron as the china plate lay on the floor in front of her in multiple broken pieces.

"Now, Mama, let me explain."

"Albert," Helen yelled to the bedroom. "ALBERT! Get out here." Albert got up from the bed, stood up to come into the main room, his shirt untucked, in his stocking feet and rubbing his forehead.

"What in heaven's ..." He stopped and broke out in a huge smile.

"Son!" He leaped over to Walter, shook his hand vigorously and grabbed his shoulder with his other hand, pulling him close. Walter stiffened again, unsure how to react, watching his mother out of the corner of his eye. Suddenly, the uniform felt restrictive.

"You've done it? You've joined the army?"

"Yes, SIR," he responded, standing up straight, almost ready to salute, his hat tipping to the side.

"Hold on a second there, Albert. You think this is good?" Helen said, still holding on to her apron.

"The best news a man could get. My son's joined the army and going to fight for our country," Albert said beaming. Walter noticed his father suddenly didn't look so tired, his jubilation taking him by surprise. That day, he had nearly worn a hole in his new shoes from walking miles around the city, anxious, a pit in his stomach, dreading his mother's reaction. He hadn't even thought about his father; but now, Albert's smile loosened the fear gripping his heart, reassuring him that he had done the right thing.

"Walter, get out of that god-forsaken uniform. Children, out of the bedroom. Your father and I need privacy." Eleanor and Claudia scattered. Helen and Albert disappeared into the bedroom. Walter stood right outside the door, not wanting to miss a word of their conversation.

"Helen. Sit down," Albert said, yet Helen remained standing in the bedroom.

"I said sit down." She looked at him with steely eyes.

She did sit down, dried her hands on her apron and starting wringing the apron cloth in her hands over and over. "Albert, please, please. Walter can't go to war. I can't lose another ... baby."

"It's outtta our hands. Our son's joined the army and going off to fight for our country."

"What if he's killed?"

"Helen, I pray he won't be killed and we'll have to pray for him every night. But men are signing up for the army left and right. Haven't you seen all the uniforms just in our building?" He paused. "You even told me about some of the sons of the suffragists ladies you work with that are going off to war, remember?" She didn't say anything but barely nodded.

Outside the door, Walter took a deep breath. "Killed?" he mouthed.

"How do you know, Albert? How can you be sure he will be protected? I just don't trust our government. Look how they've let us down. Those politicians let Abigail down by letting children work in the factory and not keeping her safe. And that was just in our neighborhood! Look how we live, all our children sleep in one bed. Look how they keep denying women the right to vote!" Helen said, waving her arms around their small bedroom, pointing out toward the kitchen and the sofa in the main room where she and Albert slept.

"Woman, this isn't about your suffragists. Don't bring them into this. Plus they've passed some new laws now for the factories. Anyhow, Helen, this isn't just about Walter. Our family needs this."

Walter's heart dropped at the mention of Abigail's name, at the memory of his mother crying and not getting off the sofa for weeks after her death, at the dark apartment that never seemed to fill with light.

"Don't you think I'm fighting for our family? I'm fighting for our children and better laws for them. We haven't changed enough laws. You know that, Albert. I'm fighting to make sure what happened to Abigail doesn't happen to another young girl," Helen said her nostrils flaring.

"God damn it Helen, this isn't about you. Nothing will bring Abigail back. Your suffragists aren't about Abigail anymore. They're for you and we both know that. Walter has to do this," Albert said, crossing his arms in a stance.

"Isn't he too young? He's only sixteen," Helen asked, her voice trailing. Walter held his breath.

"Nearly seventeen—Helen, that's practically a man. We were nearly wed at his age,"

"He needs to finish school. He can get a trade after school?" her voice getting smaller.

"Then what? War's better than any school. Besides, no one's finished school in our family. Getting a trade's a pipedream,

Helen. You and I both know that Walter'll join me in the factory sooner or later. Then what? Inhale the fumes I'm breathing, work in the dark ..." Walter cringed. He didn't want to work in the factory like his father, yet he knew it was the truth.

"When he comes home, he'll be a hero. Our family, and country, needs a hero," Albert finished.

"I can't let him go ..." Helen said. Walter, from the other side of the door, heard her breaking into sobs.

"I'm his father. I'm allowing him to go and that's final."

There was a long pause, and then "I'm his mother."

"Helen, I'm tired of watching you make decision after decision without my permission."

"What are you talking about?"

"We both know. Your work with the suffragists."

"I don't need your permission to work with them."

"Yes, you do. I'm your husband."

"Are you saying that I can't work with them anymore?

"No. I'm not saying that. I won't take that away from you. I'm saying that we're going to allow our son, Walter, to join the U.S. army and fight for our country."

Silence. Walter quietly knocked, then slipped into the room, afraid to make eye contact with his father as he sat on the bed next to his mother and began rubbing her back. Albert sat down on the bed on Walter's other side.

"There, there, Mama. It's gonna be all right. You'll see I'll be home in no time and you'll be so proud of me. You'll be bragging to all the ladies at work about your son the soldier." Helen nodded and swallowed a few times, resigned.

"I'm proud of you, son," Albert said and patted his son heartily on the back. He started to walk out of room.

"Albert, if you want this so bad, why don't you go join the army?" Helen said quietly. Albert recoiled. He looked at her and Walter, his eyes darting back and forth.

"Helen, I tried," he said softly. She looked at him raising

her brows. He took a deep breath, looked at the wall, his back now to Helen and Walter and continued, "I went to enlist but they wouldn't take me." He turned around to look at Walter and hastily added, "My lungs aren't good from years of factory work. Otherwise, healthy as a horse. It's why I don't want you following my footsteps in the factories." Walter stood up.

"I'm good, I'm good," Albert held his hand up and quickly said. "I'm probably too old son, if I'm honest with myself. You're young and have your wits about you. You'll need that over there to slay those Germans and come home safe." He then grabbed Walter and embraced him in a huge hug. Helen leapt up and wrapped her arms around Walter's other side: Walter was sandwiched in love between his two parents.

" I'll make you proud, Mama. I'll make you proud, Papa," he said.

"Just come home safe and sound," Helen said.

CHAPTER 39
Albert

"HELLO! HELLO MY GIRLS. Papa's home!" Albert said, walking into the apartment, his head lifted, full of energy, though it was the end of the day. Sauntering over to Helen, who was at the kitchen counter preparing supper, he planted a kiss on her cheek, picked up her hand and swung her around in a dance loop. His kiss caught her off guard; he rarely showed any display of affection and almost never in front of the children. Walter was gone overseas, fighting the Germans. It had happened so fast she was still in shock. Just a few months before, he had come home in an ill-fitting stiff khaki uniform, stunning them with the news that he had enlisted. Two days later, they were seeing him off at Penn Station, everyone waving furiously as he headed to basic training at Fort Greene in North Carolina. They'd gotten one letter from him rimmed with exuberance, laced with underlying tones of fear and excitement. He wrote that he was shipping out to France at the end of that week. That was the last they had heard.

Claudia and Eleanor stopped their meal preparations and stared at their father. The two children raised eyebrows at each other. "Papa is never like this, especially after work!" Claudia mouthed to Eleanor who stifled a giggle.

"How was your day today, Papa?" Claudia then asked, unaccustomed to asking him about his day.

"AAAhhh it was marvelous! Had a really interesting conversation with an elderly gentleman who was traveling to meet a cousin he hadn't seen in over forty years! The day flew by and next thing I knew it was six o'clock and time to come home. Plus, the warm breeze all day ..." he answered wistfully.

"That sounds real nice, Papa," Claudia responded, biting her lip, not sure how to react to his new enthusiasm.

"Where did you go today?" Eleanor asked. "Don't leave out anything!"

"I drove up and down Broadway all day, all the way up past 79th Street. I got to drive by the Equitable Building on Pine and lower Broadway. What a sight! I tell you, every time I drive by that building it gets bigger and bigger. It's definitely the largest office building I've even seen. I bet it's the tallest in the world!" Albert almost seemed to be preaching, standing at the pulpit, in a frenzied trance and waving his hands around animatedly. Eleanor's eyes widened as she watched his hands motioning the height of the building and reaching high to illustrate its magnitude. His status in the family seemed to be rising at the same time, ready to burst through the ceiling.

Albert's new job was the root of his high spirits. Helen could hardly believe that it had only been a little more than a month since he had first seen the posting for Streetcar Drivers in an ad in the paper one evening. He had taken to reading the paper cover to cover every night looking for any piece of news that related to the war and specifically Walter. First thing the next morning, he went down to the Third Avenue Railway System office, applied for the position and got the job on the spot. Driving streetcars for the city of New York, he was instantly standing inches taller.

"Helen, it's actually to my advantage we are at war. Most men that might've applied for the position are overseas fighting. Listen, I'd rather be fighting with our boys but look how this has worked out. I now have this fantastic new job. Maybe it did work out that I was denied entry to the army! When the war is over, I will have this job and will never have to go back to the factory!" Albert said the night he was hired.

"And then there was this sweet young couple. They were on their way to get a marriage certificate. The whole streetcar cheered when they got out at City Hall," Albert continued, sharing with his captive audience.

"Once I got past 42nd Street, I started counting horse-pulled carriages to motor cars for at least ten blocks. It was almost equal today! Not sure what we are going to do with all those horses in a few years," Albert chuckled. The way he was talking, it already seemed like a lifetime since he had switched to this new job. It had immediately become part of his evening ritual, sharing stories about daily passengers as he took his shoes off, before he read the paper and sat down to supper.

"Albert, enough with this chatter. Can you please take the trash down to the incinerator? We also need more wood for the stove while you are down in the basement," Helen asked, tapping her foot.

"Yes dear! I'll do it after supper. Any letters?" he asked. Helen shook her head.

"Well, no news is good news. I'll write him after supper. He'll be cheered up to hear my trolley tales," he said and sat down to read the paper. Helen hummed to herself as she fried the pork chop on the stove.

"Helen, did you recruit any new volunteers from the neigh-borhood for your big rally?" Albert called out from the sofa. Helen stood frozen in her spot. She shook her head.

"I'll talk to Joe tomorrow. I'll convince him to let Esther join you," he said and went back to the paper. Helen smiled to herself. Albert's newfound freedom and access to fresh air was a godsend to her as well!

CHAPTER 40

October 1917. Washington D.C. Trip #2

"WE ARE PLANNING another trip to Washington to silently picket the White House. Wilson will pay attention to us sooner or later! We need more women on this trip. I'm angrier than I've ever been. I know I've said this before, but this time it's really different. I can feel it. Who's available?" Alice Paul asked a group of women, including Helen, who were sitting around three office desks pushed together in the suffragist office in New York City. The office had changed dramatically over the last five years. When Helen first started working there in 1912, it resembled a well-appointed sitting room of a wealthy matron. Now, suffragist signs adorned the walls along with yellow-tail flags from marches and framed photographs of older suffragists like Susan B. Anthony and Elizabeth Cady Stanton, alternating with framed political cartoons that supported their movement. A few potted fern plants spruced up the desks but the chairs were mismatched, rugs layered upon one another, the cause taking precedence over design. Helen missed seeing Harriot around the office but had gotten used to her not being around. Her latest effort urged women to "go to work" since so many men were gone to war.

Dorothy, a middle-aged woman in a purple jacket reacted, "My husband said attacking the President directly is going too far."

Other women piped up.

"Will our standing in front of the White House really make a difference? He won't even know we're there."

"What if we get arrested?"

"Arrested? Can that happen?"

"Yes! A few women got arrested last month. They were released soon after. However, if I get arrested, my husband will throw me out on the street as soon as I got home!"

"He said the only women who get arrested are prostitutes and he could never show his face at the club with his wife getting arrested!"

"What would my children say if I got arrested? They'd get tormented at school!"

"I think our time is better spent working on the individual states. Look how successful the Western states and Chicago have been," someone else ventured.

Helen jumped out of her seat, "We don't have a choice! It will make a difference! I'm angry, too!" She looked at the seated women and saw them slowly nodding their heads in agreement.

What would Albert do if I got arrested? Would he throw me out as well? I don't even want to find out, she thought and shuddered.

"We can't forget about Inez Milholland! I was there back in '13 when she led the parade. For her memory," Helen exclaimed.

"Oh Inez!" a woman said.

"What happened to Inez?" another asked.

"She died last November in Los Angeles. Her family told her not to go but she wouldn't stop traveling and speaking about Women's Rights," Helen shared. She walked to the kitchen to make herself a cup of tea; Alice followed. "You must join us! We really need you there, Helen. I know how hard it was for you leave your family last time. How can we make this work for you?"

Helen rubbed the sleeves of her shirt, looked down at her shoes and cleared her throat a few times.

"I will be there, Alice!" Helen blurted out, surprising herself. How could she agree without checking with Albert? She then added, "I can only leave my family for a week this time. Can you arrange a ride?" Alice looked at her, holding her gaze a few seconds longer than usual. Helen then added, "And a place to stay?" This time around, she wasn't about to leave things to chance.

"We'll reserve a seat for you in Lucy's automobile and you can stay at The Willard Hotel with the other ladies. Glad to have you on board," Alice said as she rubbed Helen's upper arm, and then walked away.

"Thank you, Alice," Helen said, crinkling her eyes but not making a fuss. She would be riding in an automobile from New York to Washington and staying in an actual hotel! While the anticipation of that was nearly going to kill her, she nearly burst with pride that she had nonchalantly asked for a ride and a place to stay. Something she never would have dared to do even a year ago. She knew what she wanted and had gotten it.

~

A few days later, on the evening before she was supposed to leave for Washington D.C., Helen sat on the bed in the bedroom trying to focus. She was stuffing clothing into a small bag for her trip and wanted to pack as quickly as possible. She and a group of suffragists were leaving first thing in the morning. The war had become such a distraction: The suffragists had no choice but to go straight to Washington, again, and confront President Wilson—even if it was deemed unladylike.

She remembered four years ago, when she had wanted to travel to Washington for the parade, she had needed to maneuver and manipulate to get Albert's approval. In retrospect, she was still amazed that he had allowed her to leave the family at all, especially for more than two weeks: the longest she had ever been away from him and the children. None of the other women in her neighborhood left their family; she herself hadn't even traveled to attend the funeral of her father years back. Would Albert take her back so easily after this trip? This was unprecedented in her neighborhood to go out of town. When she had returned from Washington, it had taken months for the neighbors' whispers and judgmental side glances to cease. Every time she said, "Hello" to a neighbor and it went unanswered, she felt a pit in her stomach. While she cared less and less about these women, she still wanted to fit in and be part of this community, especially for her children. That seemed a smaller possibility the more she worked for the suffragists. Iris was the only one who asked about the parade and gave her a full report, confirming how well the family had fared. She had pressed Iris to share the comments from others as hard as it was to hear them.

"Wasn't she worried her husband wouldn't take her back?"

"What kind of mother just leaves her children like that?"

"She's gotten too fancy for this neighborhood."

"She can work for the suffragists all she wants, they're never going to get the vote." That one hurt the most, to hear the opposition from another woman. She could only imagine the comments and looks Albert received were even worse. But he never said a word. Didn't ask her about her trip either, but to his credit never gave her a hard time. He never stayed angry for long. This time around, she came home from work, simply asked him for permission to go to Washington D.C. He was so contented from his new job that he agreed without any fanfare. In fact, he mentioned afterwards there were rumblings of a potential union meeting for the drivers. He did say, "Just don't be gone too long and be sure to make arrangements for meals.

Claudia will be in charge?"

"Claudia, can you come in here?" Helen called out to the main room.

"Yes, Mama."

"Sit, my dear," she said, pushing aside the clothing on the bed. She handed her daughter a bag of coins and began the instructions, "Let's go over the next week. Buy what you can from the carts on Delancey Street, but there should be enough for a meat pie. Make sure you and Eleanor take turns dusting around the apartment."

Claudia nodded, rolling her eyes. "Mama, we are already doing this! I'm fifteen years old!" Claudia mocked.

Helen nodded with a big smile. "What would I do without you?" Helen asked, stroking Claudia's hair away from her face.

"Are these the new clothes from your office ladies?" Claudia asked, pointing to the clothing of rich materials contrasting on the worn bedspread.

"Oh yea ... these," half wishing she had left them hidden. They had been given to her a few months ago. She remembered the exchange:

"Helen, ummm, there will be quite a few photographers at the rally this week," Viola had stated at the office at the time.

"I know! I'm thrilled we're getting more publicity from the papers. And with photographs."

"Well, we want to make sure we look as good as we can ...."

"Of course."

"Evidently, most of the people reading the papers are men. And ... they are the ones controlling the vote to grant *us* the privilege to vote."

Helen nodded, her eyes growing smaller, turning her face downwards not wanting them to see her flushed cheeks.

"It can't hurt if we look as attractive as possible in the photos in the paper."

Helen looked down at her plain brown skirt.

"We are in awe of how you lead us and everything you do: recruiting a constant stream of new volunteers, organizing the rallies, and then attending every event," Viola paused. "A few of us here in the office put together a bag of fashionable attire that we think is your size." She started to pull out item after item and held it up for Helen to admire. Helen stood there, shrugging her shoulders. They were exquisite pieces that she never would have aspired to own.

"We just want to attract as much positive attention as we can and it will only help if we look as attractive as possible. You know Helen, you are a beautiful woman ..." Viola reached her hand out to touch Helen, brushing her hair slightly, causing Helen to flinch backwards.

"Thank you," Helen mumbled. She took the bag home that evening and stuffed it under the bed in the bedroom until one day, Eleanor had come out "dressed up" in one of the outfits.

"Mama, Mama, don't I look pretty?" she said, twirling around. The shiny silk skirt and bright white cotton shirt brightened up the dull dark apartment. The polished materials reflected off Eleanor's face. *These clothes do bring some light around here,* Helen thought. From that moment on, she put her pride aside and incorporated the lavish new clothing into her daily routine. She knew that these items were cast-offs and last year's fashion to those women, but to her they were a glimpse of a better life.

Now, getting ready for her trip, Helen looked at the outfits on the bed, rapidly grabbed a handful of outfits and crammed them into the small bag. "Can you make sure Papa cleans the stove and gets fresh wood to light it?"

"I'll try Mama ...."

Helen hugged her daughter, whose sturdy arms felt strong around her neck.

In the kitchen, Albert was reading the paper.

"Albert."

"Hmmmm."

"I'm getting ready to go," Helen said. Ever since Walter had been shipped overseas, Albert devoured the daily newspapers, following the war to every minute detail. Today was no different. He put it down with an exasperated sigh.

"I'm leaving for Washington first thing in the morning. You know that, right?"

"Yes, for the thousandth time, Helen. I still don't understand why you have to go on another trip. How long will you be gone?" he asked.

"Just a week. Albert, the last trip I took was four years ago. Picketing the White House seems to be the only way to get President Wilson's attention! I feel honored they included me. You are set then? I'll be home before you know it. I promise," Helen said.

"Yes. We survive fine without you," he said and went back to reading the paper. He folded it closed and grabbed another one underneath, scanning the articles with his finger. She didn't argue with him because he had a point. She was around the home much less, spending most of her time at the suffragist office. Claudia was more of a surrogate mother to Eleanor: taking care of the shopping and cooking, picking Eleanor up from school, even doing the washing. Eleanor wasn't such a little girl anymore at eleven years old! Helen attempted to clean the apartment at night but often just cleaned the surfaces as she barely had the energy.

"What's the news?" she asked, glancing over his shoulder to see the paper.

"Walter's letter said he was somewhere in France. There's nothing in here about battles in France. Seems most of the fighting is still in Germany. I can't wait to hear his stories when he comes home."

Thank Goodness he's still in France! Even though we have no idea, she thought, pressing her lips together. Every night she prayed that Walter would never see the front lines, though that was what Albert seemed to want. It wasn't enough that his son was a soldier, he had to come home with war stories, too; Albert was living vicariously through their seventeen-year-old son. She still was in disbelief that Walter, still a boy, was so far away and could get killed at any moment. When she thought about losing another child, she felt a hot flash.

"Are you really traveling in an automobile?" Albert asked. Ever since the "Grand Picket" had happened, when more than 1,000 women had marched around the White House in icy, driving rain on the eve of President Wilson's second inauguration, Alice Paul had become insistent that they picket the White House non-stop. The public didn't approve of the picketing, which incited her even more; it had become hard to get her attention. Her determination that Helen join the picketing was emphasized by arranging to journey to Washington in an auto.

"What kind of automobile is it?" Albert asked, arching his back and looking up at her; it was the first question he had asked about the trip.

"I'm not sure ..." *He seems more interested in the car than why I'm going,* she thought. "I promise to come home with all the details and also write Walter all about it. You know how crazy he is for cars!" she answered, placing her hands on his shoulders. "I hope he's getting our letters, but who knows? I won't stop writing."

"Where you staying?" Albert asked, stretching his arms over his head.

Helen paused. Alice had arranged for them to stay at a hotel, her first one.

"The Willard Hotel." Albert just nodded his head.

"All right, I'm off to sleep. Alice is picking me up very early tomorrow morning," Helen leaned in to give Albert a peck on the cheek. "I do love you very much ..." she said quietly. He looked up at her, making eye contact.

"I hope you'll miss me," she said and leaned in to hug him. "I promise to make it up to you when I'm back. You'll see, I'll be back before you know it. Thank you again for letting me go, Albert."

"I will miss you, Helen. We'll miss you," he replied. Helen burrowed her head in his neck, inhaling his scent she knew so well. She got up to bid goodnight to the girls in the bedroom.

"Ellie, Claudia, I'm leaving before dawn tomorrow morning and won't want to wake you," she said as she tucked the blanket around their legs. "I love you both—more than you'll ever know! Remember, Claudia is in charge, my little one," she added, hugging Eleanor extra tight and planting kisses all over her nose.

The next morning, Helen dressed in a new outfit: cream silk shirt, navy blue woolen skirt and belted camel coat; without waking anyone, she then walked down the stairs of her building, hoping she wouldn't run into any neighbors. The automobile pulled up with Alice Paul, Lucy Burns driving, and another passenger, Mabel, in the back seat.

Lucy leaned her head out the window and called out, "Helen, get on in. We're going to Washington!"

CHAPTER 41
En Route to Washington D.C

HELEN WAS SITTING in the backseat of the automobile.

"Is this a new automobile?" Mabel asked.

"Not really. It's my brother's, but he wasn't using it. He's been traveling so much; he told me to take care of it while he was gone."

"What kind of car is it? I'm not an expert, it's more my husband's pastime. He gets quite annoyed that I don't show interest in his hobbies and am involved in my own interests," Mabel continued.

Who has time for hobbies? Helen thought.

"It's a Ford Model T, I think. Quite pleasant to drive. Even though we are using it for the cause, I'm elated to get the chance to take it out on the open road and give it a whirl!" Lucy then turned to Alice, her expression more serious, "Do you expect many other women to show up?"

"We have about ten to twelve committed, but I'm not sure. With the war at full steam, even our ardent supporters seem afraid to antagonize their husbands or seem anti-war," Alice answered, lowering her eyebrows.

Typical Alice— her dedication ... never married, no children. Helen thought for a moment what that would be like. She did love Albert and couldn't even imagine her life not being married or not having children. She and Albert had drifted apart when Abigail had died; but the love for their children and Helen feeling more fulfilled had brought them back to each other. She felt his disappointment with not being able to enlist. While she felt conflicted about Walter being overseas, seeing how happy it made Albert actually soothed her on a daily basis.

An hour into the ride, Helen had barely said a word; she just listened and looked out the window. She saw sheets of green: trees blending together; ribbons of red, brick homes; streaks of brown and thatched roofs in one long line; the towns indistinguishable from one another. She couldn't smell the smoke from the fireplaces in the homes or steel burning from the factories they passed. The automobile was going too fast. While she loved the idea of the trip from New York to Washington taking only twelve hours, the speed felt unsettling. She had nothing to hold on to. She could now understand Walter's fascination with automobiles.

It was much past supper time when they finally pulled up to the Willard Hotel in Washington D.C., right on Pennsylvania Avenue. All the women, including Helen, kept tucking loose strands of hair back into their buns and under their hats after the hours they had spent sitting in the automobile.

"Miss Burns. Welcome. Pleasure to have you return," the doorman said as he opened the car doors and immediately reached for the bags tied to the back of the car.

"Is the kitchen still open?" she turned to the doorman.

"I'm sorry Ma'am but the kitchen is closed. We do have cold food available: cold chicken, bread and cucumber salad, I believe. Would that suffice?"

"Why yes, thank you."

"Please, head to the dining room. We'll take care of your automobile."

This meal will cost what we spend on food for the week, Helen thought as they all walked into the lobby. The lights were dimmed yet the tall marble columns leaped out and led her eye to the ornate painted decorations on the ceiling. At least a dozen single lamp chandeliers hung from every few squares.

The four women went straight to the dining room, sat alone and ordered the food the doorman had mentioned; as it was past the typical dinner time, there were no others in the room.

Helen was famished, but noticed that the other women picked at their food. Helen wished she could rip the chicken apart and devour it; it was unlike anything she had eaten. Even cold, it was moist, with crispy skin, fatty and tender, not like the dry stringy meat they usually ate at home.

"Alice, do you remember when President Wilson walked by? He even tipped his hat at us to acknowledge our presence?"

"Yes, I do. It was more bemused condescension. Somewhat encouraging. He did invite us for coffee." Her expression changed, her smile disappearing. "I don't think we amuse him any longer. With the war fully engaged, we are almost seen as … this time we are doing it different. I've coined it the 'Silent Sentinels.' We are protesting with our bodies not our voices. We've been coming here for months and we are back now. I'm determined not to leave until something changes! We are protesting to Wilson and the White House silently!" She continued, "Well. Let's get a good night's sleep and rest up for tomorrow. I have a feeling we will need our energy," she said as the other women nodded their heads.

Helen went to sleep that night in her own hotel room tucked under a goose feather filled blanket, but she still couldn't sleep. The room was cold; since the war was on, even posh hotels like this one were struggling to get enough coal for heat. More than the cold though, she was worried about picketing, which seemed so different from a parade. Had she made a mistake coming?

The next morning, groggy from tossing and turning all

night, she walked with the group to the White House, all of the women wearing purple, white, and gold sashes: the colors of the National Women's Party. Recently, they'd separated themselves from the Congressional Union for the Woman Suffrage party and these colors were a way to differentiate themselves as a result of their militant tactics.

Helen adjusted her gold sash and unfurled a banner she had made in New York.

"Mabel, Lucy, here are your banners," Helen said, handing them over, then unfurling her own: "Mr. President, what will you do for woman suffrage?"

Then she handed Alice her banner—a bit tentatively. Alice had picked the quote herself, which read: "Kaiser Wilson, have you forgotten your sympathy with the poor Germans because they were not self-governed? 20,000,000 American women are not self-governed."

"Alice, aren't you worried the crowd will jeer at us?" Helen asked, fidgeting with her glove.

"Why?" Alice asked. Helen pointed to the words "Kaiser Wilson."

"They might. But I'm tired of playing nice and being polite. That has gotten us nowhere. It's not what I learned in England with Emmeline Pankhurst. Let them boo and hiss at us! We are remaining silent. They will finally realize we are serious."

Helen stood in front of the White House, the iron gates looming above making her feel fragile and insignificant. The twelve women standing together didn't say a word, didn't shout out their normal sayings and chants, sticking to their self-imposed "Silent Sentinel" mandate. Still, a crowd soon formed around them, with the usual sneering men.

"Look at these floozies."

"You ladies belong in the looney bin."

"A few months ago, when we were here picketing the White House, they were very respectful but I'm afraid the tide is turning," Alice whispered and kept her head high, looking over the crowd. The comments grew from the crowd.

"Ladies, get your heads out of the sand. Don't you know there's a war going on?"

"How can you be so unpatriotic?" a woman shouted, walking by.

How can another woman say that? Helen thought.

Alice shouted back, "We're not unpatriotic. In fact, this woman's son is fighting overseas for our country," she said, putting her arm around Helen's shoulders.

The female attacker backed away but the hostile and defensive feeling lingered. Helen gasped when Alice broke her silence, especially at her defense. She felt uncomfortable to be singled out. If she had her choice, she would never have let Walter enlist, no matter how happy it made Albert. She couldn't stand the thought of losing another child. Her heart would never mend from Abigail's death; it always lingered.

As the day wore on, the insults became louder and the mob grew angrier:

"How dare you picket our President during wartime?"

"Did you hear, they called our President 'Kaiser Wilson'?" a man yelled to the others, his angry gestures contrasting with his fashionable bow tie, plaid jacket and straw hat.

"Girls. Put your fight to rest. It's never going to happen."

"There is a boat leaving for Berlin with room for you on it. Go join your co-patriots."

Lucy Burns whispered, "Keep quiet. Nothing we say will make a difference. Our presence is enough." Alice nodded. Lucy continued, "Remember we are the 'Silent Sentinels.' We cannot afford to have anyone arrested today. We've already had enough of our ladies carted off to jail. This doesn't bode well for keeping and recruiting volunteers."

Alice nodded but then said in a quiet yet powerful voice. "I agree, but I won't forget the Pankhurst methods."

"What's she talking about?" Mabel whispered to Helen. Helen leaned into Mabel's ear and said, "Alice learned her suffragist tactics from Emmeline and her daughter Christabel Pankhurst. They were famous suffragist activists in London. Let's say they were much more militant than we are and often fought with the police."

"I don't think I could do that," Mabel said, shuddering.

"Me neither, but I never thought I would picket in front of the White House and here we are," Helen said, holding her sign up higher, jutting her chin out, with a gleam in her eye. She added, "I should be anxious about being arrested, but I'm not. We aren't doing anything wrong," she added.

Later, Helen started to shiver as the sun began to set. She was feeling the chill air and hoped that Alice would give a sign that it was time to head back to the hotel.

As if on cue, Alice said, "Ladies, let's wrap up our banners. We need to preserve our energy—we might be in Washington longer than I thought."

Helen felt her chest tighten. *How long does she mean?* she wondered. *I can't stay away from my family for more than a few days!*

CHAPTER 42
October 1917. Iron Gates

"THE CROWD WAS, well not what I expected," Lucy Burns said, trudging in her two-toned ankle boots. Alice, Lucy, Dora Lewis, Alice Cosu, and eight other women walked ahead. Their group had grown to now nearly twenty women with more women arriving throughout the day.

"Were they like that last time?" Helen asked.

"Oh gosh no! We had a few rowdy men per usual but on the whole they either walked by or expressed passing interest. Today, they were ... Well, they were downright nasty!"

Helen nodded, the pessimism sinking in.

"Who's minding your children while you're gone?" Mabel asked.

"Minding? Oh, they're minding themselves I suppose. Their father is home, too," she added, almost an afterthought.

Helen didn't have the nerve to ask Mabel about her staff at home supporting her on this "adventure." She envisioned Mabel would come home and all would be neat and clean and running smoothly. Helen's home was never clean, there was never enough time.

"I'm sure tomorrow will be better. Let's remind ourselves of the marvelous memories of the parade: how many women showed up to march and how many people cheered us on all day," Mabel said dreamily and linked her arm through Helen's as they walked into the darkened lobby of the Willard Hotel, the lights dimmed to conserve energy for the war effort. Helen appreciated the quiet—no one would be shouting at them here.

"Let's meet in the dining room in forty-five minutes for supper? I need to freshen up," Lucy Burns suggested, and the group scattered.

Helen sat in the lobby for a moment, a little disoriented. She did not usually freshen up before supper. She supposed it couldn't hurt to tidy her hair, use the restroom, wash up. However, she was afraid to go up to her room lest she collapse onto the bed and miss dinner. Instead, she stayed in the lobby, where she nodded off thinking that if she were home Eleanor would be sharing funny stories from her school day, Claudia would be asking about the suffragists, Albert would be poring over the newspapers looking for an update on Walter and she would run to the mailbox looking for a letter from her son. The women walked down the stairs, looking much neater.

"Helen, Helen. Time for supper." Helen felt a hand gently shaking her awake.

Fancy for dinner, even after our long day? Helen thought, as she looked at the women heading into the dining room, smelling floral scents as they walked by, noticing their fresh application of lipstick, face powder, their hair combed and buns redone, yet still wearing their sashes.

"I've just telephoned Gordon. He still seems upset that I'm here in Washington picketing," Mabel shared. "How did your husband handle your trip?" she asked Helen as they walked in together.

"Surprisingly, he didn't give me a hard time. I wasn't sure if he would let me go after the parade in '13. But he seemed to understand that we had to be here. He's hoping we don't get into the papers. I didn't tell him I hope we do!" Helen said.

"You're lucky he's so supportive," Mabel said. Helen acquiesced and thought *I guess I am luckier than I thought.*

The women sat down, taking up five tables of the dining room, and barely spoke at dinner; they were beaten down by the ongoing barraging comments of the unsympathetic crowd from picketing. The other female diners were dressed in fashionable evening wear, even given the wartime conditions: flattened bust on a dropped waist, loose-fitting straight-cut dresses hemmed to the mid ankle. Most were adorned with decorative large clips and pins. The men joined them in formal evening wear of white bow ties, coats with tails with white kerchiefs sticking out of their breast pockets. They all gave the suffragists sideways glances, looking right at their sashes.

"What're you ladies here for?" their waitress asked them as she served their after-supper tea.

"We're suffragists," Lucy answered.

Helen saw the puzzled look on the waitress's face and piped in, "We are working to get women the right to vote. We're picketing the White House trying to convince President Wilson."

"Good luck to you, ladies. Could be a while," she said, laughing out loud and walking away from the table, clanking the dishes balanced on her tray.

Later that night, in her room at last, Helen undressed and thought about the last time she had been in Washington, for the parade four years ago. She and the other suffragists had felt confident and hopeful. Now, it felt as if there was an ominous cloud hanging over her and her fellow picketers. The twelve-hour journey had passed so fast from NYC to Washington, there had been no time to allow the gravity of this expedition to seep in.

She crawled into the plush bed, burrowed under the covers to warm up and felt achiness in her legs and joints. Was she tired from the day? They hadn't walked much but standing in place for 14 hours was even harder on the body. She prayed she wasn't getting ill, tossing and turning, unaccustomed to the softness of the mattress, the multiple pillows and silky sheets.

Then, suddenly, she sat up, crying out loud, "I miss him!" She grabbed a pillow and hugged it close, her eyes suddenly flooded with hot tears. Her body throbbed, recalling how she and Albert nestled together, the rhythmic turning over at the same time due to the narrowness of the couch, and inhaling the scent of his skin when she needed to connect and be reassured. Except for her trip to Washington four years ago and a handful of missing nights when Albert didn't come home, they had slept together every night for the last seventeen years. At that moment, her body was telling her their connection was stronger than ever. She didn't want to be single like Alice. She loved him so much her heart ached.

The next morning, the women, refreshed from a good night's sleep, were back at the gates of the White House early. Within fifteen minutes of their arrival, three policemen approached them, swinging their sticks in anticipation of a fight.

"Beat it Ladies, go home," the first one barked.

"The President instructed us to ask you to leave," a second one bellowed.

"We have every right to be here," Alice responded, keeping her head down, not making eye contact.

"Well, it looks to me that you are obstructing traffic," the first policemen answered.

"No, we're not. We're right here on the sidewalk and haven't stepped foot on the street," Alice answered.

"What's that banner say?" the third policeman asked, poking at Lucy's banner. Helen held her breath, thankful he didn't poke Alice's "Kaiser Wilson" sign, knowing how it would incite them.

Alice read out in a loud crisp voice: "We shall fight for the things which we have always carried nearest our hearts: for democracy, for the right of those who submit to authority to have a voice in their own governments." She added, "It's from a speech President Wilson gave to Congress."

"Lady, you've got no right to use the President's words out here!" the second policeman charged, his voice quickly raised.

"It's a free country. Sir."

"I don't know about that. The President instructed my Chief to keep an eye on you ladies. Now, if I see any more commotion that is obstructing traffic, I'll arrest you without a moment's notice. You've been warned," and they walked away.

"Alice, I've never heard the police be so rude," Lucy commented.

"You should hear them in my neighborhood. This is how they normally speak to the people where we live," Helen added.

"I've never been spoken to like that," Dora Lewis said.

"They clearly see us like they do in my neighborhood. It doesn't matter how polite we are, they look at us like dirt," Helen said.

"I had no idea. How do you put up with it?" Dora asked.

"Put up with it? We have no choice! They're the ones in control," Helen said with a sad smile. "Before I became a suffragist, it never even crossed my mind to question authority. Albert had, at one point, joined the labor union and was trying to organize them in his factory. I did everything in my will to fight him and convince him to stop," Helen said, noticing the group of women were listening to her every word. "Now that I'm a suffragist, every day it is confirmed for me that I have no choice but to be a suffragist. But mind you, I'm one of the few women from my neighborhood who has joined up and definitely the only one here," she said waving her hand at the group. The women listened, spellbound.

"Well, we're doing nothing wrong. In fact, I've decided to stay a few more days. Who can stay with me?" Alice asked the group of suffragist picketers.

"I'll stay with you. I'm not ready to leave yet. They need to keep hearing our message," Dora Lewis said.

In unison, most of the women, except for Helen, answered, "We're staying with you Alice. We're not going anywhere."

"Helen? What about you?" Alice Paul asked. Helen looked at Alice, frozen. She envied the women who could stay and picket. Waiting for them at home were nannies, maids, cooks and housekeepers: tending their children, cooking their meals and cleaning their homes. Yet on the other hand ... she had traveled so far, finally gotten Albert's permission to go to Washington and Claudia was plenty competent to handle shopping at the street food carts and dusting their small tenement apartment. Would her family even notice as much if she was gone for a few more days? This opportunity to stay in Washington would most likely not present itself again.

"Yes, I'm staying," she answered. Alice reached over, patted her arm and she felt warmth emanate from the other women, who were smiling at her.

CHAPTER 43

Arrested

THE NEXT MORNING, they followed what already seemed like a routine: leaving the hotel early, dressed in their sensible shoes ready to stand for eight hours. They walked in silence, noise from the street drowning out their thoughts with their heels clacking on the sidewalk, carrying their rolled-up signs under their arms. But when they arrived, they were greeted by a group of policemen dressed in thick blue wool double-breasted short jackets standing just a few feet from the spots they had occupied the last few days. The policemen looked like they were waiting for them.

"Good morning, ladies," a baby-faced policeman called out. None of the women responded. Instead, Alice, her head held high, adjusted her sign, a different one, which read: "To Ask Votes for Women is Not a Crime." Helen looked at the younger policeman, who reminded her of a younger version of Albert. She saw his handlebar mustache quiver and noticed his fingers clutching and unclutching the shiny wooden nightstick attached to his belt. But the women held their ground, positioning themselves as close as possible to the White House gates, their backs touching the cold iron of the 12-foot-high fence as they slowly unfurled their banners. Within a few moments, the group covered a significant portion of the gates, their bodies and signs shielding the White House entrance from people walking by.

The baby-face policeman walked over immediately, his supervisor nudging him, and tapped Helen's banner with his stick. Her sign read: "Vote Yes for Women Suffrage" with a big box with an X marked inside.

"Ya can't be here, Lady."

"Why not? I'm not doing anything wrong," Helen answered in a polite yet strong tone that was firmer than she actually felt. If Abigail could see her now. She was so different from the woman/mother that Abigail had known before she died, the woman that had tried to pull her daughters back from that first suffragist parade. Abigail would never get a chance to see the woman that Helen had become: someone willing to stand up to a Washington D.C. policeman in front of the White House. She wanted to remember every detail of this uniform to recount the story to Claudia when she returned. They would sit at the kitchen table laughing at the scene. Albert would jokingly admonish her but she would feel his pride. She might even write Walter about it to lift his spirits while he was on the front line in France fighting the Germans. They were both fighting for freedom after all!

"Ya, you are, Lady," he answered.

"What's that, Sir?" She threw in the "Sir" hoping it would appease him, that he'd just turn around and leave them alone.

"We told you ladies yesterday you couldn't be here."

"We haven't set foot on the street, like you asked. We're not obstructing anything," Helen answered, trying to recall their exact words from the day before. Within moments, three other policemen crowded around her poking at her sign, forcing her to move toward the curb until she found herself, unwillingly, standing in the street. Seconds later, two policemen grabbed her on either side, squeezing her arms so hard she dropped her banner, which they promptly trampled on. They were dragging her toward a black patrol wagon with "Police Department" written on the side. She dragged her feet in front of her, digging them into the street, then lowered her body so her bottom nearly touched the sidewalk. It slowed the policemen down but they were still inching toward the wagon. Her arms in a vise-like grip, she lifted her legs and started kicking the policemen holding her. One of them slapped her across the face so hard, her cheek felt on fire and her eyes welled with tears. Her face stung.

"Let me go!"

"C'mon Lady! You're going with us."

"I haven't done anything wrong!" Her cries drowned out, they didn't slow their pace nor ease their grip on her arms. Helen looked up and gasped at the pandemonium that had erupted. Lucy Burns was holding onto the iron gate of the White House that they had all been standing in front of just moments ago with two policemen trying to pull her off. She, too, kept kicking at the policemen while holding onto the gates. Another policeman had his arms wrapped around Mabel Vernon's waist and was literally lifting her off the ground, walking towards the police wagon. Alice Paul held her head up high and didn't fight the policeman on either side of her, looking elegantly as they escorted her towards the wagon. It was hard to believe that just early that morning they were walking to the White House, cautiously hopeful with a sense they were making a difference. The few people that had been protesting them scattered immediately and no one was left to watch this unconscionable treatment.

Within moments, Helen was sitting inside the small police wagon next to a dozen other women. The policemen slapped handcuffs on their wrists right before they pushed them into the van. Their bodies were jammed up against each other in a tight space, with no room to move.

'When I was arrested in New York last year, they dropped

the charges right away," Alison Turnball Hopkins said.

"Harry said, if I end up in jail again, I might as well not come home," Mabel piped up, her voice breaking. Helen had heard other arrest stories from women and they wore it as a badge of honor. Helen sat with slumped shoulders and felt faint. Albert could easily throw her out of the house when he found out she was in jail. He wasn't a huge fan of the police either, but his wife getting arrested might push him to the brink of an irrational decision. He had always said he would support her work with the suffragists up to a point. They had never gotten around to discussing what that point was. Getting arrested now seemed like that point. Where would she go? Iris could only take her in for so long. Her mind was spinning. This seemed to be a fate almost worse than death. Was this what Abigail had died for, that Helen would end up in jail?

"Alice, Alice. Where are they taking us?" Helen asked, trying desperately to remain calm, feeling the metal handcuffs dig into her wrists. The more she moved them around, the deeper the marks and restraint. She was afraid she would throw up even though her stomach was empty from not eating all day.

"If it's like last time, they'll scare us at the police station, put us in a holding cell and we'll be out by tomorrow morning. Their tactics don't work."

Helen felt a small sense of relief that she'd be out by tomorrow morning and en route to New York as soon as possible. She'd walk home if she had to. There had to be another way she could serve the suffragist cause without ending up in jail. She had much more to lose compared with these other women.

Maybe I'm not cut out for this. This is too much, Helen thought.

After being left in the cold wagon for hours, true to Alice's word, they were processed at a police station in Virginia and placed in a holding cell. As the winter sun set, Helen heard other women's stomachs rumble as well; a lone policeman appeared at the holding cell door.

"Thank goodness, they've come to their senses and are letting us out."

"I wonder if Joseph's attorney came through."

"At least they are taking us seriously," Alice said.

Helen looked at her and thought, *Is she galvanized by our arrests?*

"All right, Ladies. Time to go," the policeman grumbled, not making eye contact. Helen followed the other ladies, with a spring in their steps: they were being released! However, multiple policemen appeared out of nowhere, slapping handcuffs on the all the women—again—and dragged them back to the same police wagon parked in front of the station.

"What's going on? Where are we going?"

"We demand to know! Tell us immediately!"

"We have rights! We didn't do anything wrong."

"Please, let me call my husband," Claire said as she burst into sobs, her will finally broken down.

Helen's knees nearly buckled; she wasn't sure if she could walk. But she straightened out and followed the crowd again. This day was becoming more and more of a nightmare and she kept praying that she'd go to sleep, wake up in the morning and be back in her musty tenement apartment that was home.

The wagon took off straightaway and within an hour they pulled up to an imposing stone gate which went all around the daunting building: a guard stood with a large rifle wrapped around his chest waving the wagon through. The policeman driving looked back at the women, "Welcome to Occoquan Workhouse."

Is this what hell looks like? Helen thought.

CHAPTER 44
Prison

DARKNESS FELL SO RAPIDLY, Helen could barely see the other women with her. The wagon stopped abruptly and they were led into a large drafty empty room with cabinets against the wall and high-barred windows, manned by two daunting women guards. The women crowded together, sticking to a corner far from the guards, making the room seem vaster. The female guards wore neckties, similar to a man, thick black wool jackets with a shiny badge over their flattened breasts, and their hair pulled back taut, causing them to appear even more severe.

"Miss, can you take our handcuffs off?" Alice Paul asked. Helen moved her wrists around, the metal digging in deeper.

"I didn't give you permission to speak," the guard said. Every breath of air left Helen's body; this was not a good sign.

"You ladies refused to pay the fine and now you're in jail: Occoquan Workhouse," the other guard said.

"We weren't given a choice to pay a fine! I would've paid it," Mabel cried out.

"Why would we pay a fine? We're innocent and didn't do anything wrong," Alice said.

I couldn't have paid the fine even if I'd wanted to, Helen thought.

"Get undressed now," the other guard bellowed as she

walked around unlocking their handcuffs. Helen looked around agitatedly, trying to see what the other women were doing. She had never been naked in front of anyone besides Albert and her children.

"I said NOW," the guard yelled. The dozen women in the room stripped slowly, each piece of clothing revealing further vulnerability. First came the lace-up winged ankle boots, then velvet and wool jackets came off, belts clanked to the floor, and long-sleeve cotton blouses were shed. Helen kept her eyes low but saw corsets falling to the floor; she was the only one in the room without one. They peeled off the long winter tights until they stood in just their slips.

"Everything ladies!" Slowly but surely the women removed their slips and undergarments: silken, lace, variety of pastel and cream colors blending together, compared to Helen's faded off white until they were all standing naked. Their arms covered their breasts, pubic area, and even faces.

"Line up." The women followed instruction. The two guards proceeded to inspect every crevice of their bodies treating them like hardened criminals that would hide knives and other forceful objects between their buttock cheeks. After not finding one inanimate object, they were taken to a showering station and forced to bathe with just one bar of soap to share among the dozen women that had clearly been used by other prisoners. Many women refused to use it. Afterwards, they were handed a baggy blouse and long shapeless skirt made from material that resembled flour sacks Helen saw at the general store, boots most likely left over from the men's prison and long itchy woolen long underwear. All the clothing smelled rank and unclean.

"No undergarments?" Dora asked. No one answered. When they were all dressed, the women were given a hair tie and ordered to keep their hair pulled back as tight as possible at all times. Looking around the room, Helen now saw haggard, worn-down women who just that morning had been wearing large ornate hats, blouses, jackets and coats made from soft wool in rich hues and leather shoes fit perfectly to their feet. They looked like two completely different factions. They were escorted to cells that fit six women. Each of their cells had a few women residing, either sitting on a cot or hanging by the bars. Helen found herself with two black women, who right away, approached her.

"Why you in here lady?" She didn't answer.

Lucy Burns, who was in her cell, responded, "We didn't do anything wrong. We're innocent. We were arrested for peacefully protesting at the White House. We are suffragists."

The black women looked at her confused. "Lady, we all did something wrong."

"What did you do?" Lucy asked.

The two women laughed. "We're prostitutes! Just trying to earn a living," and went back to their cots chuckling. What would be worse for Albert to find out: that she was in a cell with black women or prostitutes? She prayed he would never find out either!

Lucy leaned over and whispered, "It's just a tactic to humiliate and coerce us to pay the fine. It won't work. We'll wait for the pardon, it'll come. Last time, it came after three days.

Three nights I have to sleep here? Helen thought. She couldn't speak. She sat on the cot, holding her face in her hands and held back tears, afraid if she started crying she wouldn't stop.

This is too much, I'm not cut out for this. This is not how I thought I'd end up working for the suffragists. Will I ever get out of here? she thought.

CLANK. Startled, she looked up and trays of food were being shoved under the bars. The six women walked towards the trays: colorless slop, watery tea and rock-hard dark bread. In the corner was a pail of water that looked to be their only source of water supply.

"There's a worm on my tray," Dora said, also in their cell. None of the suffragist women ate. It had been just hours before that they were eating their breakfast off bone china at the hotel in Washington.

After a sleepless night, the women woke up to a barrage of multiple guards taunting the women.

"You'll see. Your husbands won't take you back after you've been in jail."

"Do you know how terrible you women smell?"

"You can't run away from us. We will find you."

Ultimately, they demanded over and over the women admit their guilt, yelling, "You'll get out if you pay your fine." The suffragist women stuck together, proclaiming their innocence.

To make matters worse, the women could barely eat the food.

"I don't recognize any of this food."

"I don't think you can call it food," Mable said, in tears, worn down from the guards' verbal abuse.

By the second day, the combination of the unheated cells, thin blankets and drafty halls, all caused their strength to wane dramatically. Their protests weren't as strong, even down to a whisper; they lay on their cots longer and some even ate the food.

Alice Paul proclaimed, "I'm going on a hunger strike." As soon as the guards heard about it, they threw her in solitary confinement. For days thereafter, Helen waited for her, their fearless leader, to return but she didn't.

"Is she dead?" she hesitated but then asked Lucy in a hushed tone in their cell.

"Of course not, she's stronger than that." Lucy answered. Helen vacillated between wanting to be rescued herself and breaking out of her cell to save Alice.

CHAPTER 45
Night of Terror

"BRUTALIZE THE ... Those ... ladies." Helen heard the words clearly, sitting in her cell. If she hadn't, she might've thought they were a mistake. But there was no mistake, those were the exact words Whitaker used when he was giving orders to the male guards, while he trolled up and down the hallway in front of their cells, not talking to the women and barking his order to the guards. Whitaker was the superintendent and used his power to orchestrate the guards to perform any action he wanted taken, even if later deemed atrocious. When he first welcomed Helen and the other women the evening they arrived, there was no way they could have foreseen the terror he would instill. Yet that's what these new male guards did: brutalize the ladies, just like monkeys obeying their master. These new male guards were brought in to replace the female guards that had been working there before.

The night was November 14, ten days after they had gotten to the prison. Helen would never forget the date: it would soon become a "Night of Terror." After she heard the lone sentence Whitaker spoke, guards started appearing out of nowhere. If she had hoped to be rescued before, those feelings were now desperation for the guards to disappear.

The guards walked around with cigarettes hanging out of their mouths, throwing them on the ground, stubbing them with their heavy-duty leather boots, then lighting another one right away. The wood-paneled floor became a large ashtray marked up with brown residue. The scent of cigarettes mixed with offensive ashen smell caused Helen's eyes to water.

One guard appeared. Another guard. Helen smelled the cigarettes and felt her heart beat out of her chest. She counted five cigarettes.

Some guards had uniforms with knee high boot, provoking an even more fearful aura. They ranged from young fresh-faced barely shaven men to older men with gray trim beards.

"These ladies aren't sleeping tonight," Whitaker yelled at the guards as they started their rampage. The guards turned around and followed the orders by attacking the women.

"Get this tramp off her cot."

"Her hair isn't pulled back tight enough."

"That hobo didn't look me in the eye." Then the physical assault began. Helen saw Dora Lewis dragged into the dark cell opposite her cell. She couldn't see anything but heard a hard thump against the iron rail of the bed.

"Please, please, STOP. NO ... Momma Momma ...."

She prayed it wasn't Dora's head causing the thump but the cries of anguish caused her to fear otherwise. She soon smelled the metallic scent of blood wafting from the cell.

"Dora? Dora?" Helen asked quietly. No response. Please let her only be knocked out and soon wake up.

Helen sat shivering, from cold and fear, on her thin mattress, pulling the dank rough woolen blanket over her threadbare uniform. She waited, holding her breath, afraid to make too much noise, dread in her stomach. Her cell now had only two other women: the black prostitutes. She could only see the whites of their eyes as they were huddled under their blankets as well.

"Gee whiz, didn't expect such feisty dames here," one guard muttered to the another.

"Can't wait to get out of this slum and away from these Bug-Eyed Bettys," the other said, nodding his head in agreement. She heard them join two other guards where they entered the cell of Alison Turnbull Hopkins and Mabel Vernon. A few minutes later, new cries of distress traveled down the hall for everyone to hear.

"He's choking her. Make 'em stop," cried out Mabel. Helen heard fists pounding against cloth, and assumed Mabel was punching the guards to make them stop choking Alison.

"Hold her down. I'm done with this feisty Betty," said one of the guards, not even making an attempt to keep his voice down. A moment later, Helen heard a belt unbuckle and the clap of pants falling to the floor.

"No, please no, I'm begging you, please don't ..." it sounded like Mabel's voice.

"I'm next, hurry it up," Helen heard another belt buckle clank as it fell to the ground. Helen and the whole cell block could hear Mabel whimper, her paltry protests and the guards panting and grunting. Finally, Mabel was quiet and the guards picked their pants up from around their ankles and buckled their belts.

"Get dressed and keep ya mouth shut," one of the guards snapped at Mabel.

"They don't even go after us like that," her black cell mate quietly shared.

Helen was afraid to move, didn't want the guards to notice her. Afraid she'd be next to assault. However, she didn't remain unnoticed. Three guards she didn't recognize barged into her cell. They didn't speak and grabbed Helen from under the blanket. Two guards each seized an arm. She was so fearful, she didn't want to antagonize them any further so didn't say anything. She was afraid if she started begging, she would get raped like it sounded Mabel did. She closed her eyes and thought, *Please God- don't let these men touch me or hurt me. I promise to be a good wife to Albert and stay home for my children. Please God. Please God. Please God.*

With her eyes shut, she couldn't see what they were doing. They lifted her arms over her head and then chained her hand to the cell bar over her head. They kicked her a few times in her hip and leg and she did everything she could not to cry out from the excruciating pain. Staying quiet was the only way these guards might not attack her. She opened her eyes and saw them walking out. Even when the guards weren't smoking, their foul cigarette odor stuck to their sweaty wool uniforms.

Her hip throbbed, sending pain spasms up and down her leg, but she felt a huge sense of relief, dodging an attack for now. The rest of the night continued with guards grabbing the suffragists, dragging them, beating them, choking them, pinching and kicking them. Helen heard the cries all night from the women, begging them to stop the physical and sexual assaults. Then silence. No one ended up coming back to her cell.

The next morning, the female guards were back on duty. While they didn't terrorize the women like their male counterparts, they weren't doling out any sympathy either. Helen's arms were so numb she couldn't feel them still chained to her iron bed. A guard simply walked into her cell, unlocked her from the chains and walked out. Her wrists were achy with deep red welts; she could barely move them around. The aftermath resembled a bloody battlefield: women lying on the floor, bruises already forming, blood pooled on the splintered wood floor, chained to the iron bed rails and cell bars, some doubled over with broken ribs and limbs, and some knocked out left for dead. A few women were taken to the infirmary for dressings.

Later that day the women gathered for the mid-day meal, helping out the ones who couldn't walk as easily, surveying the damage. The women were sobbing silently, afraid to antagonize the guards.

Lucy was especially inconsolable but was able to spit out, "Alice Cosu didn't survive. I saw her lying there in the infirmary. She had a heart attack and didn't survive," she said between sobs. Helen put her arm around her, not sure what to say.

"Did you see Dora?" Helen asked. Lucy nodded.

"She's alive. Miraculously," she said.

"It is a miracle she endured that beating," Helen said, thinking of the guards raping and beating her, and Dora's cries. "I'll never forget her cries," she added. Women around their table nodded, all having heard the atrocities. Helen looked at the red burn marks on her wrists, wondering how she pulled through fairly unscathed. During the night, Helen had counted forty guards, yet there were only 33 suffragist women imprisoned.

"Is Alice still in solitary confinement?"

"Yes! And she's still on her hunger strike."

"How long has it been?"

"Five days! They are bringing in the people to force feed her!"

Gasps were heard all around.

CHAPTER 46

Coming Home

BY THE END OF November, two weeks after the Night of Terror, the women were released from the Occuquan Workhouse Prison. Their lawyers came through and argued that since they were arrested and sentenced in Washington D.C., it was illegal to place them in a Virginia workhouse. Worse for the wear, they returned to their respective homes, mostly in New York. Helen was no exception, riding in a car, exhausted, her hip and leg in pain from the guard's kicks that hadn't healed properly. But she was alive and hadn't been violated like some of the other women. She turned her worries to Albert's reaction to her current state.

Helen tottered into the apartment and observed the dismal state: unwashed dishes, open empty cupboards, dusty floor and piles of dirty clothing. She had been gone for nearly two months. Disappeared from her family's life. Did they think she was dead? Were they already mourning her? Were they holding on to a glimmer of hope that she was still alive? Did anyone from the New York suffragist office reach out to Albert or Claudia? Had everyone simply forgotten about her?

She collapsed on the sofa, alone for the first time in months, unsure if she was safe. It was midafternoon and Eleanor, Claudia and Albert would be home soon. She was desperate to see them but grateful to have these solitary moments to let it sink in she was really home. Even though she had gotten out of jail after 60 days, she didn't feel rescued. No one had come to liberate her. Yes, they did end up releasing her and the other suffragists. But what they endured, well ... she was home now, that was all that mattered. Or was it? She placed her hat over her face, shut her eyes and waited.

Claudia entered the apartment with Eleanor in tow and stopped in her tracks. "Mama? Mama?" she ran over to Helen, fell down on her body, heaving sobs, hugging her. "You're home. You're home. We didn't know ... we didn't know ..." barely getting the words out. Helen's hat fell from her face and she felt exposed, sullied, afraid to make eye contact with Claudia and Eleanor. She didn't want them to see her in this state. She was afraid her gaunt face, matted hair and sunken eyes would scare them off. It didn't matter. Both girls were on top of her, hugging her, crying, placing kisses all over her dirty face, not letting her go. She couldn't look them in the eye yet but felt the tightness in her chest slightly ease and her breath resume a bit. Her guard lowered, and she joined their sobs.

Claudia stood up, untied Helen's boots and unbuttoned the same coat that she had put on when she left the apartment nearly two months ago.

"What happened, Mama?" Claudia said. Helen finally looked up. Claudia was standing over her and Eleanor was lying on top of her—both staring at her. Albert wasn't home yet from his job.

"We thought you died, Mama. Just like Abigail," Eleanor said.

Helen broke out in sobs again and hugged her tighter. "I'm here now. And not going anywhere again. I promise."

"You have to tell us. What happened?" Claudia demanded.

"Not yet, Claudia. Soon, I promise," she knew she'd never be the same and would have to eventually share but she wasn't ready yet. She had done *nothing* wrong. All they were doing was standing up for what they believed in: women having the right to vote. They weren't breaking any laws, they were peaceful and not doing anything violent. It wasn't fair that such horrible things were done to her.

What if things had turned out differently? What if Abigail had never died? She continued to lay in silence, letting her daughters' warmth seep into her skin and rejuvenate her. Hours later, she heard Albert's thick footsteps down the hall and walk in the door. Claudia ran to him while he was still in the doorway and they spoke in hushed whispers. Helen couldn't hear but moments later, she felt Albert remove her hat. He started stroking her forehead, rubbing his fingers at the temple of her hair, just the way he knew she liked it. She had expected him to run over to her like the girls had, but he kept distance. Did he know what happened to her? How could he have known? Was her sullied appearance keeping him at bay?

"You're home, Helen."

Helen took a deep breath but didn't say anything. She wanted to talk to him, sit up and hug him but she was so exhausted. She took a few deeper breaths, closed her eyes and fell asleep.

She woke up, disoriented to a darkened apartment, only a low gas light was lit on the kitchen table. When she sat up, Eleanor ran up to her. "You're awake. You missed supper."

"I guess I did."

Claudia placed a plate of that evening's supper, toast spread with minced ham and canned string beans, on her lap. "Mama," she said and grabbed her hand, "Please, tell us what happened."

She shook her head, "I don't know...."

"I'm here ..." Claudia said, stroking her arm. Helen just shook her head, tears streaming down her face. She looked up and Albert was sitting in a kitchen chair, watching her.

"Claudia, why don't you put your sister to sleep? Your

mother and I need some privacy," Albert said, tight lipped, clenching his fist. When they were alone, he asked, "Helen, where were you? You were gone two months!"

"No one contacted you?" Helen asked, sitting up straighter.

"No."

"Albert, I was arrested. We all were. They jailed us unfairly. We weren't able to contact anyone. Many of the women tried to call their husbands, lawyers. Finally, one of them got us released and I came home immediately," she relayed in a quiet voice, not wanting her daughters to hear. She patted next to her on the couch, "Albert come here, sit next to me, please," he shook his head.

"You went to jail?" he asked in a raised voice. She looked down at her stained clothing and nodded her head slightly. She felt even dirtier.

"Albert, I had no idea we were going to get arrested. If I had, I never would have gone to Washington," she said, remembering the screams she heard all night during the Night of Terror.

"I don't know Helen, I don't know," he said shaking his head slowly from side to side.

"You don't know what?" she asked.

"I don't know how I'll be able to live with a woman that was in jail. My wife arrested! You're tainted. Damaged goods. Not respectable anymore," he said. Helen felt like she was choking, couldn't breath and started hyperventilating.

"Albert, you can't mean that!" she whimpered.

"You've let down your family. Me, the children. It was bad enough you were away from us for so long. How are we going to live with the shame and embarrassment? It was bad enough that I was pestered about you being a suffragist. But this, it's too much." he said.

"Would you rather I had died? I thought I was going to die," she pleaded. He didn't answer.

"I need you to leave Helen. Get out," he said crossing his arms.

"Where will I go?" she asked. He shrugged his shoulders. She finally got up, put her boots back on and clutched her coat.

"Was it worth it, Helen? Was fighting for the suffragists worth it?" he asked. She stared at him and then shut the door behind her.

Helen went straight to Iris's apartment. When she opened the door, Iris looked at her, her face went white. "I thought you'd died!" she cried out and grabbed Helen in a tight hug.

Helen sank into her arms and said, "Albert threw me out."

"You can stay here for a few nights but—" Iris said, stepping back. "Come on in, let me put some hot water on and make you a cup of tea. Tell me everything, where were you for starters?" Iris said, leading her inside. Helen shared the whole story.

Iris's response was, "Oh I don't know how Albert will get over this. It seems different this time."

Over the course of the next few days, Helen stayed with Iris and her family: three big boys and Iris's husband. It had been tight before and Helen knew she couldn't stay much longer.

Iris shared that when Helen was gone, she had helped Albert and the girls quite a bit.

"How did they seem?" Helen asked, desperate for any morsel of information.

"Oh Helen, they missed you of course! We didn't even want to think that you weren't coming back," Iris said while they tidied up the apartment.

"How am I going to convince Albert to take me back?"

Iris was sweeping the main room then looked up at Helen. "It might be a while, but he'll take you back. That man loves you to pieces. He won't be able to live his life without you. Trust me," then went back to sweeping.

Helen raised her eyebrows and Iris added with a tight smile, "It's not the same with Ed and me. He's happy when I cook but he never looks at me the way Albert looks at you. You might have to give up the suffragists though."

"I can't live without them. And I definitely can't live without my girls! Now where am I going to sleep?" Helen asked looking around. Iris pointed to the floor and said, "I'll look for an extra blanket."

CHAPTER 47

Getting into the Newspapers

HELEN WAS STILL NOT allowed back into her home. She could barely eat and hadn't gained the weight that she had lost in prison. It was killing her to still be away from her family. She stole moments with her daughters when Albert wasn't home and before he came home from work. But he was still extremely angry and they hadn't spoken since she had come home from prison a few weeks ago. She tried repeatedly but he wouldn't let her in. She could hear Claudia and Eleanor crying behind the door imploring him to let her in but to no avail. She couldn't stay more than a few days with Iris. With a stammer and blinking back tears, she had to go into the suffragist office and ask one of the ladies if she could stay there. She was hailed as a heroine as one of the prisoners and several women volunteered to take her in. The truth was that most of the women had extra bedrooms anyhow. She ended up staying at Viola's townhome tucked in a side street near Grammercy Park. She couldn't appreciate it, though, and all she yearned for was to be home with her family in the tenement apartment. She kept thinking about what Albert asked, "Was it worth it? Was fighting for the suffragists worth it?" It still was but would she give them up now if she couldn't get her family back? Hopefully she didn't have to make that choice. In the meantime, to distract herself and to get the message out, she focused on telling their prison story to the public.

Helen stepped off the streetcar at Bryant Park and looked around: office buildings lined the streets, businessmen promenaded around, the New York Public library loomed resplendent in front of her and with only a few apartment buildings—in contrast to her neighborhood downtown. She hadn't spent much time north of 34th street and immediately felt out of place. She was inundated by the scents on the street: tobacco from the Natural Bloom cigar store, paint from the Hardware store and sour beer from the Bryant Park tavern. Sordid men milled about a storefront advertising furnished rooms. Feeling uneasy, she wished she could pick up her pace but her hips were stiff and her leg dragged since she had come home from prison, not allowing her to walk as easily. She stopped to focus, take a deep breath and figure out where she needed to go: the Tip Top Luncheonette, two blocks away on West 40th Street.

As soon as Helen arrived, her mouth watered from the sign outside advertising a hamburger special. The smell of grilled fatty meat wafted through her nose causing her stomach to rumble, but the 20 cents price stopped her in her tracks: she couldn't spend that. Even if she had the extra money, she wasn't sure her stomach could handle it. She had barely kept any food down since her return: her stomach was consistently upset. She had to walk around the men standing outside, engrossed in their daily paper, so she could enter.

"Influenza Fatal to 62 More at Dix!" read a newspaper headline.

"Helen, here," Carol Green waved at her from inside mouthing the words. She was sitting at a table with another similarly fashionably dressed woman. The women had planned to meet at the Luncheonette to update each other on reporter contacts: Carol and the other woman had taken the reporter outreach very seriously. They insisted she join them for the lunch, knowing that Helen's firsthand account would entice the reporter even more to write a story and perhaps feature it prominently in the newspaper.

When they invited her to lunch, Helen hadn't known how to respond; she had never gone out to lunch, especially with women like this. Her face fell as she entered the Luncheonette, squinting her eyes to adjust to the darkness. Inside it was dark and crowded with tables close together; there was barely room enough for the waitresses to walk between tables and serve the food on their trays teeming with sodas, open-faced sandwiches and toasted muffins. There was a dusty cloud swirling around, indicating the sawdust-covered floor was overdue for a sweeping. She had expected these women to dine at a more upscale establishment. She had only ever eaten in restaurants since working with the suffragists and this eatery did not match the others. They were sitting with a man she didn't recognize: his hair was slicked back tight and shiny and he was smoking a cigarette. Even Helen recognized that his suit, while pressed, was too shiny to be expensive and his tie too narrow to be tasteful. His pointer and thumb fingers were yellow from nicotine. Helen heard them talking as she approached the table.

"I'm tellin' ya, this is a great story. Great story." He paused to take a drag from his cigarette. "I read some of the accounts in the other papers but I need a firsthand story. I'm counting on yours today. If you dames weren't so serious, I'd think you were making it up," he said, taking another drag on the cigarette.

"Wait until you meet Helen Fox and hear directly from her what happened," Carol said. "Here she is," Carol looked up and smiled at her as Helen took a seat. The man barely gave her a glance.

"Helen, this is Dale Brody. He writes for *The Evening Standard*." He finally looked at her, gave her a quick nod.

The waitress came up to the table and asked Helen, "What'll you have?"

"Just a malted milk." It was only 3 cents. She really had to watch her spending now that she only had her paycheck.

"Is that it, Helen? The open-faced turkey meal is divine," Carol remarked.

Helen shook her head and offered, "I ate a big breakfast."

"Tell me everything. Don't leave one juicy detail out. I want to make sure I include everything in the article," Dale said as he lit a new cigarette with the butt of his short stub that was still smoldering.

Helen looked at Carol, all of a sudden uneasy and unsure she could actually share the sordid details of what happened inside the gates of the Occaquan Workhouse. Would he accept her statement as truth? She barely believed it herself sometimes and wondered if it had all been a horrible dream. But then she would get up to get a drink of water and feel the pain shooting from her hip down her leg and knew it was all true.

"They treated us like prisoners, even though we hadn't done ...."

"Speak up, I can't hear ya," he barked.

"We hadn't done anything and ...."

"What?! What'd ya say?" he barked again. Helen cleared her throat. Was she really going to be able to divulge to him the grisly report he was looking for? She bowed her head so her table companions couldn't see her eyes well up. She was terrified, but knew she had no choice and would have to share the account of what happened to her and the other women in prison. The outside world had to know. They had heard some of the stories but they needed to hear the whole truth. Even if at first they didn't believe her.

"Take your time. We're in no rush," Carol said, placing her hand on Helen's back and handing her a starched scented linen handkerchief. She used it to dab her eyes.

"Mr. Brody. You cannot imagine the traumatic incidents Helen and the other ladies unjustly encountered in prison. She will share her experience but please don't harass her," Carol admonished. Dale sat back in his chair, giving Helen some space.

Helen felt herself calm down and no longer felt as weepy. She began to speak with a low voice. While Dale didn't say anything, he leaned inward to hear her. Carol patted her back, a sign to speak up if she could.

Helen spoke louder. "Even though we hadn't done anything wrong, we were immediately treated like the worst criminals. They demanded we pay a fine and confess without any other information. Of course, we didn't! They wouldn't let us contact our family so no one knew where we were. My husband and children thought I had died. They took our dignity away by forcing us to undress in front of everyone, taking us to a showering station where we had to strip naked and bathe together. Afterward we were placed in cells with prisoners who had committed crimes and they served rotten food infested with worms." Dale sat there grinning, writing furiously in a pad and shaking his head. He balanced a cigarette in his lips, spoke, wrote with a pen, seamlessly moving the cigarette from his lips to his hands over and over, all at the same time. He stopped writing and looked up at her.

"Anything else? Was that all that happened?"

Helen looked down at the malted milk. Would he believe her? She sat on her hands to stop them from shaking. She was afraid what Albert would say when he saw the article in the papers. Would he be even more ashamed of her?

"No, that's not all that happened." Even though the luncheonette was packed with diners, noisy with clanging dishes and people coming and going, their table was heavy with silence. They sat frozen awaiting Helen to continue speaking.

"Next our night of terror happened," Helen said.

"I like that: 'Night of Terror,'" Dale said, writing it down then giving her his full attention.

"Go on," he said quietly. Helen looked at Carol who nodded her head and gave her a tight-lipped smile.

"It started with the male guards ...."

"Male guards?"

"Yes. We had only had female guards up to that point, but Whitaker, the superintendent, brought in male guards for that night. For the sole purpose of torturing us. And torture us they did. They beat us, kicked us, chained us to the beds and to cell bars." Helen showed her wrists, which still had scars that would never fully heal. Dale was now feverishly writing again, not wanting to miss a detail. She continued sharing the stories of the women who barely survived that tormented night and ones who had survived but were abused more than the others.

"I heard one of the ladies died, but I didn't know all this," Dale said. "What about Alice Paul?" She already had a heroic reputation in the media.

"Alice wasn't there that night ...."

"She wasn't? Wasn't she in prison with you?"

"Her story is worse," Helen drawing out her words.

"She was in solitary confinement. At first, they gave her nothing but bread and water but then she went on a hunger strike which really angered Whitaker and the guards. They then brought in a physician to force-feed her. I don't know if I will ever forget those cries ringing in my ears—we all heard the screams throughout our cells, ringing in our ears for days. I actually heard the physician say 'Alice Paul has a spirit like Joan of Arc, and it is useless to try to change it. She will die but she will never give up.'" The table was quiet and no one asked any more questions.

"Eventually they placed her in a sanitarium in hopes of declaring her insane and finally released her when we were freed."

"It's a miracle she survived," Carol said.

"She told me that singing saved her. She sang every song she could remember from childhood. If she couldn't remember the words, she made them up. The guards would yell at her to quiet down but she didn't. Towards the end, she was so weak and couldn't walk as much but she kept singing."

Dale sat up straight in his chair and took a deep breath. "I'm telling ya, they are going to eat this up. My editor is not going to believe me."

"Will he not publish the story then?" Helen asked.

"Nah. He will."

"Mr. Brody," Helen asked in a quiet voice.

"Call me Dale."

"All right, Dale. Will you include the reason why we were in prison?" *That's the whole point ...* Helen thought.

"Yeah Lady. I know about your cause. I get it, I get it. The thing is, we want to sell papers. That's my job and that's the only thing my boss cares about. The story of you ladies in prison will sell lots of papers. Why they got there, ehhh, I'm not so sure," Dale said.

"What Helen is trying to say, Dale," Carol put her hand on Helen's hand, "is that we understand you have to do your job. We are just trying to do our job as well. If you could include at least one or two small details about women having the right to vote, we would greatly appreciate it." Carol smiled and touched her hair for emphasis.

"Sure, I get it," Dale said. Helen had a lot to learn about subtle negotiations from Carol. She took a sip from her malted milk, the first sip of the egg cream felt uneasy on her tongue.

"If it's not too much trouble, we would like Alice Paul and the other women to be called political prisoners. They really were, you know. Of course, feel free to mention as much as you like of the despicable specifics of their prison stay, such as the unhygienic conditions, forced labor, meager and unsanitary food ..."

"Hold on, hold on, this is good, slow down. I gotta write it all," Dale couldn't keep up with Carol's salacious accounts.

"... the contemptuous and violent treatment the women received from the administrators and finally, don't forget about the forced feedings of the strikers!"

"All right, ladies. I got enough here," Dale stood up and tapped his notebook with the cigarette. "This is a story. Great story!" he added and walked out. Helen wished that the story would be favorable and would wear Albert down to let her come home. She just hoped it wouldn't work the other way and he would be so embarrassed it would anger him even more.

CHAPTER 48

Jan 1918. Headlines

HELEN WOKE UP EARLY, got dressed swiftly and went downstairs to the kitchen in this new house she was staying in. She heated up leftover coffee from the day before, afraid to bother anyone. She didn't mind day-old coffee anyhow, never letting food go to waste. She added a drop of condensed milk to cut the bitterness of the chicory. She woke up every morning nauseated and it didn't go away until she went to sleep. It seemed it would never go away while she was estranged from her family. She left the house, rushing to the newsstand, and was soon holding up the *New York Times* which carried the headline: "WILSON BACKS AMENDMENT FOR WOMEN SUFFRAGE."

Helen jumped up and down, "This is important. Very important! It's everything I—we've—been working on!" she said out loud to no one in particular. She then grabbed a copy of The Tribune and read, "SUFFRAGE WOMEN PRISONED AND TORTURED!"

"I've got to get home and show this to Albert and the girls!" she said again out loud.

Oh Albert, she thought and her face fell. *He has to take me back. He has to!* She ran as fast as she could, even with a throbbing hip, all the way home. It was still early and soon she was banging on the front door.

"Albert. Albert! Please let me in. I've got news!" He opened the door already dressed in his driver uniform.

"What is it Helen?" he asked, baring his teeth.

"I've made the papers. We've made the papers," she said breathlessly holding it up. She showed them the headline and drew attention to a picture of Alice Paul on the cover.

"I got this into the paper!" She then pointed back to the *New York Times*. "Because of the imprisonment story, we've been able to convince President Wilson to vote for the Suffrage Amendment."

Helen quickly scanned the article and then read out loud: "President Wilson ... came out squarely for the proposed amendment giving women the right to vote ..." Albert took the paper from her and scanned the article, nodding his head slowly, pursing his lips. "Ahem. I see," he murmured.

"This is noteworthy," he said and looked up at her.

"Albert. Can I please come home?" she pleaded. Claudia and Eleanor peeked out from behind him. "Please Papa. Please?" they begged. Albert looked at Helen directly in her eyes.

"How can I take you back? Do you not realize how you've shamed yourself? Embarrassed us?" he said pointing to himself and the children.

"Albert. I truly didn't mean to. If I had known I'd get arrested, I never would have gone to Washington," she implored, shuffling her feet back and forth. "I know it doesn't undo the shame I've caused you but good has come out of it," she added nearly inaudibly, pointing to the paper. Albert looked at the paper and looked at her, his eyes darting back and forth. Helen squeezed her eyes shut.

"There'll be changes," he snorted.

"Yes. Yes. Changes," she answered practically hugging herself.

"You can't go out of town anymore," he said slowly.

She grabbed both his hands and exclaimed, "YES YES! I promise never to go out of town!"

"And, I also want you to cut back on your work with the suffragists. I'm making more money now," he added.

Helen let out a deep sigh. "Yes, Albert. I understand. I'll work less," she responded, darted into her home and hugged her daughters until they were laughing and crying falling onto the ground, planting kisses on each other's noses, cheeks and foreheads.

That evening, Albert brought home the paper that he normally read: *The Evening Standard*. True to his word, Dale Brody got the Occoquan Workhouse imprisonment account as a major story in this paper. As Helen had predicted, many other newspapers picked up the story as well. He read the story after supper and remarked, "This prison sentence really sounds terrible. It will be great for folks to hear about this. Well, no one should be treated like that, man or woman. It also says that Alice Paul was issued an apology by the National Association Opposed to Woman Suffrage from …" he stopped to look up the name, "a Miss Minnie Bronson."

"That was the news we were hoping for," Helen smiled and grabbed his forearm. She was about to say more but stopped herself. She had compromised but didn't have a choice. She still was allowed to work with the suffragists. Later than evening as she lay in bed next to Albert, her stomach finally full from a wonderful supper with her family, it now seemed worth it.

CHAPTER 49
Jan 1918. Public Outpouring

"MISS ALICE PAUL, Chairman of the National Women's Party and leader of the militants who picketed the White House made this comment: 'It is difficult to express our gratification at the President's stand. For four years we have striven to secure his support for the national amendment ....'"

Alice went on to read from an article in the *New York Times*: "Democratic Congressman from Suffrage States became alarmed ... they fear that if the resolution were defeated by Democratic votes, women ... would go over in droves to the Republican candidates next November."

"I actually believe they want us to vote," Alice said. Helen looked at Alice, her hair in a no-nonsense loose bun at the nape of her neck, wearing a navy blue, velvet dress with a lace v-neck collar. Even coming off a prison stay that would have caused most women to stay in bed for months, she looked elegant and poised.

"I truly believe the reason they haven't granted us the right is—simply, we are a pawn in their political games," Alice said. Helen sat next to her at a table in the National Women's Party office in New York. They had spread out all the newspapers that had been covering the stories. Since Helen had started the public relations campaign, the press was eating up the suffrage cause. Nearly daily, there was a headline in a paper covering them. Helen didn't really understand the power play that Alice was discussing and the politics seemed so complicated. Her sole concern was making sure the Suffrage cause stayed in the paper and kept them on the forefront.

"Aren't you offended by the word 'militants?'"

"No, not at all. I'm proud of our tactics. I am still in shock, and recovering from being in jail and the horrific tortures. We all are—look how thin you are. But I'm proud of what we've done and the message we've gotten across. This war is dreadful as well. We've wasted so many years because of the war," Alice said.

Helen said a silent prayer that Walter was on his way home. They hadn't heard from him in so long but also hadn't gotten a notice that he had died. At this point, she still felt that no news was better than nothing.

"We can't let them forget what happened to us! We've got to do more," Helen exclaimed, almost frenzied.

"Yes, yes! We can't let them forget. Did you hear about the 'Prison Special' railroad car?" Lucy asked. Helen shook her head.

"A few of the women that were arrested have rented a railroad car to go around the country. They are calling it the 'Prison Special.' They want to keep public attention on the suffrage issue, especially in the Senate," she said.

"Prison Special! That's unusual!" someone said, laughing. The rest of the women in the office laughed.

"Yes, we need all the help we can get in the Senate. That is proving to be tougher than we had anticipated," Alice chimed in.

"I didn't feel so special in prison. But … if it gets people to talk about our cause, well, then it sounds like a good idea,"

Helen said cautiously. She tried to join in the laughter but couldn't. She still had nightmares about her experience there.

Over the next few days, hundreds of letters flooded the office. Helen sat at a table surrounded by them. She couldn't get enough of the letters and ate each one up hungrily. It seemed to temporarily satisfy an insatiable appetite for confirmation of her role.

"Listen to this," Helen said holding one up, "Mrs. John Simon in Greenwich, Connecticut writes, 'I am aghast that something like this could happen in our great country of America. While we are fighting the Germans abroad, we should be uniting and supporting our women back home. My husband and I plan to write to our congressman immediately. God bless you all.'"

"I hope she got to her congressman sooner versus later. The House of Representatives is due to vote on the woman suffrage amendment this week," Alice said archly. "It's in today's paper," she tapped a copy of the *New York Times*.

"Read another one, Helen. Are there more like that?" someone asked.

"Yes. 'Please find attached $1 to support your suffrist cause. I had no idea you women were fighting so hard for my rights.' Signed Mrs. Calvin March." Helen continued to read quotes from the various letters as dollar bills and coins dropped out of the envelopes she opened.

"Helen, you had so much to do with this public support," Maude said as she looked through the letters with Helen. Another woman walked in with a large bag of new letters that had just been delivered.

"It's true. Because of all this press," Alice said and waved her arms at the stacks of letters, "we have an appointment with an influential lawyer next week. He wants to help get the charges against us dismissed," she added.

The success of the public relations campaign did help confirm how critical she was to the cause. However, she didn't feel she could take as much credit as they were bestowing on her for the advancement of the suffrage movement.

CHAPTER 50

Going to the Movies

SALLY ADJUSTED AND PINNED her hat with one hand and held
the door for Helen with her other hand as they left the suffragist
office on 23rd Street.

"And then we went to a matinee on my day off," Sally said.

"A matinee?" Helen asked.

"Yea. We go every chance we get. Don't always have the day
off or money but when we do ..." she stopped and shook her
head smiling. "They're only 10 cents."

"Which one?" Helen asked.

"We love the Charlie Chaplin movies—our sides hurt from
laughing. But doesn't matter, we'll see anything playing. Well,
I'm off. Back to work, Mrs. Fox. See you next time I'm off,"
Sally said.

"When will that be?" Helen asked.

"Who knows? When the Missus gives it to me," and briskly
walked uptown.

Helen had run into Sally at a meeting at the suffragist office;
she was a maid who had gotten involved in the suffragist movement and Helen was one of the only people she connected
with at meetings and rallies. She wasn't always around because
she couldn't get away from work often. However, she was dedicated. Whenever she had a free moment, her time was given

to the suffragist cause with a rare date here and there with her dejected beau.

If Sally can go to the cinema, then why can't I? Helen thought. *I never do anything like that. Or anything fun. I don't really have the time. But neither does Sally. But she doesn't have children.* This circle of thinking kept looping in her head over and over until she got home.

"Albert, we have to go to the cinema!" she called out as she burst through the front door. Albert looked up from his paper and said "Nah ... that's for the women folk."

Helen felt too buoyed to let his dismissal get her down. "Fine if you don't want to go. Claudia, let's go to a matinee. This Saturday. I'm not working and you don't have school."

The next Saturday, Helen and Claudia made plans to go to a matinee, a first for both of them. They still hadn't convinced Albert to join them. Helen had stayed up late the previous evening and gotten up early that morning to clean the apartment from top to bottom: washing the floor, cleaning the sheets, even preparing a meal for that evening. They were still repairing and making up since he had allowed her to come home after her prison stay. He had complained before that she didn't cook as much now so she went out of her way to only cook their meals and not serve any store-bought food. She was working less as she had promised, so it worked out anyhow. As she was peeling potatoes for a shepherd's pie—Albert's favorite dish—she asked innocently, "If you don't want to come, can you stay home with Eleanor?" She knew it would be easier for him to agree after he had seen her staying up late and up at the crack of dawn cleaning and cooking for him.

He looked at her and answered, "Yah, but be sure to come home early." Helen nodded her head and smiled in agreement. Inside, she was fuming. She was well aware of their agreement and didn't need a constant reminder. But it was the deal she had made.

"You know, Mama, you are not like any other mothers that I know, in the building or my school friends' mothers," Claudia said as they were walking to the movie theatre that afternoon. It was biting cold outside and they had linked arms to stay warm against each other. When Claudia had looped her arm through Helen's on their walk for warmth, Helen felt a rush of tenderness go through her. As soon as she heard this comment, she started to stiffen.

Uh oh, here goes. I'm about to hear what a horrible mother I am. Never at home, never cooking meals, never sewing… Helen thought. "What do you mean?" Helen asked, not wanting to hear the criticism about to come. They were embarking on her first leisurely activity in—she didn't even know how long—and it was going to start on this negative note?

"Some of the women do work, in factories or stores. I counted the other day; at least five of my friends at school had mothers that worked. In fact, Franny's mother works as a janitress in their building. That doesn't sound like a fun job. She doesn't have a choice since their papa died," Claudia said.

"No, it doesn't sound like it," Helen said. She was already thinking what her response would be.

"Well Claudia, we wouldn't be able to go to this matinee if I wasn't working."

"Well Claudia, we always have enough food. It's not fancy but it's enough for all of us." Truth was, she worked because she loved what she did and couldn't imaging not working for the suffragists. It was the main reason she got up in the morning.

"And the mothers that don't work, well, they seem to be working so hard, just at home. They are always cleaning apartments that never get clean enough or cooking for more mouths than they had planned or even making too little food stretch out a long way. They seem pretty miserable if you ask me."

Where the heck is she going with this? Helen questioned.

"I know what it's like to clean an apartment that never seems clean," Helen retorted. "And ... I know what's it like to stretch a meal that isn't enough food for too many mouths."

"Mama, Mama," Claudia said as she patted her mother's arm, "you do clean and you do cook, when you can. What I'm trying to say, is when my friends and I were talking about our mothers working, I realized you are the only mother I know who seems to be working in a job she loves. You have a smile on your face when you come home most evenings. You usually have a story to tell ...."

Claudia kept talking but Helen didn't hear anymore. She felt her body relax and her face redden with warmth. She was thankful they were walking at a steady clip with her hat pulled down low to block out the cold so Claudia wouldn't see how flushed she was.

Maybe this feeling of never doing a good job, at home or at work, was worth it. She usually felt like she was letting someone down, whether it was her family or Alice Paul and the suffragists. But maybe she was actually a good mother after all.

CHAPTER 51

Walter

HELEN BRAIDED HER HAIR and lay in the darkness, waiting. She wasn't ready to go to sleep. An hour passed. She undid her hair and then braided it again. She looked at Albert's side of the bed and wondered where he was and when he'd be home; she pulled the blanket more tightly around her. She felt the cold more keenly now, since prison. She leaned over to smell his pillow and inhaled his scent: musky and sharp. She thought about the last few months since she had been released: they had settled into a routine that was comfortable enough for both of them, a truce of sorts. He had stopped being angry about her being in prison and she accepted that working less was better for her health as well. She was still working. It was an eerie sense of calm for the first time since Abigail had died more than six years ago.

She heard his cautious footsteps on the faded hallway carpet, barely covering the splintered wooden floorboards. He was treading lightly so not to wake anyone up but it was past midnight and most people in the building were sleeping. It was hard to sneak in at this hour. Still dressed in this streetcar driver uniform, with his back turned to her, he took off his worn leather brown boots, trying to not wake Helen up.

She sat up. "Where were you?" she asked in her gentlest

voice possible. The fact that she could ask him his whereabouts directly showed that trust had returned. The last few weeks they had been speaking to each other with respect, asking about the other's day. Albert was even pitching in with chores.

"I came from a meeting," Albert answered.

"A meeting? What kind of meeting? You didn't tell me you were going ...."

"I know. I tried but there never seemed like a good time. The Amalgamated Transit Union had a meeting tonight. More and more of the men at work have joined. I wanted to hear what they had to say."

"But Albert ...."

"I know Helen, I know," he said, holding his hands up as if holding her back. "They could fire me if they knew. Or at least make my job extra hard—take away hours—give me the lousy routes. I had to go ...."

"And ...?" she asked.

"They shared the minutes of the recent meeting with management and the terms they asked. They are asking we all get paid a minimum wage and sick leave if we are hurt on the job. Remember Joe? His streetcar got into an accident that was not his fault and now he can't work. The union's trying to get him paid but ...."

He stopped speaking and said quietly, "Aww, you're shivering." He came to the couch and sat next to her, rubbing her shoulders vigorously to warm her up.

"What if you lose your job? I want to keep working but some days my hip and leg hurt so bad from the ..." This union membership could be very favorable, but she also was terrified.

"Helen, change is coming, whether I'm part of it or not," he responded with a thoughtful smile. "We're in this together. I just want to be able to take care of you and our children," he stated, hugging her closer.

"Changes are coming, we don't have a choice," he repeated and continued getting undressed and ready for bed. "This is my time, Helen. It's our time."

The next evening, Albert sat at the table looking over some papers, flyers and agreements that he had received from the union. He had decided to go forth and join and was trying to understand the paperwork. They heard a knock at the door. It sounded heavy and focused. Everyone stopped what they were doing and looked at the door, caught off guard.

"Were you expecting someone, Albert?" Helen asked.

"No. You?"

"No." They all sat there. No one got up to answer the door. They heard the heavy knocking again a few moments later.

"Albert, please, can you answer the door?" Helen asked. Her knees were weak and she couldn't stand up. She had such an uneasy feeling.

Albert opened the door and saw a man, really a teenager, dressed in uniform. He took his hat off and put it under his arm.

"Mr. Fox?" he asked.

"Yes." The uniformed man saluted. "I have something to give you."

Helen held her breath. She sat there frozen. She had replayed this scene over and over in her head dozens of times. She had also witnessed the screams from other apartments in the building and heard stories of soldiers delivering fateful news from other people. It was inevitable that it was now their turn. The time had finally come.

"Your son, Private Walter Fox, will be arriving home shortly. He is alive but injured and will be stationed at the New Haven hospital in Connecticut. Here are all the details."

Helen burst out in tears. "Walter is coming home! He's alive!" She leaped up to hug Albert and they both stood there sobbing with relief.

CHAPTER 52

Claudia

"CLAUDIA, make sure you dress extra warm today. The almanac predicted freezing temperatures this week," Helen said as they cleaned up the breakfast dishes. Though Claudia was doing all the washing and drying while Helen stood next to her leaning on the small counter.

"How's your leg today, Mama?" Claudia asked.

"Hmm. Not better but not worse," Helen responded. Claudia was really running the house, Eleanor was increasingly independent at ten years and Walter was finally home. It had been a harrowing two years with barely any word from him—many months Claudia knew her parents spent sleepless nights wondering if he was alive. Then he came home and had taken months to recuperate up at the hospital in New Haven. He had been shot in the leg by a machine gun and shrapnel fragments from the shell had infected the area. But he survived and just had a small limp. He was one of the lucky ones. His now quiet demeanor made him appear much older than his barely nineteen years. Papa was still digesting the fact that Walter was studying to be a teacher but Claudia was proud of him.

"And wear your sturdy shoes," Helen added.

"Which ones would those be?" Claudia said grinning, she only had two pairs, both scuffed and much in need of a decent shoe shine. They had a low heel making them even more unfashionable; not narrow as the ones most women wore on the streets these days. These only had laces while buttons were the rage.

"The dark brown lace ups. We're going to do a lot of walking up Fifth Avenue today. This march is planned throughout Manhattan, walking the whole way."

"I know Mama. We went over the plans last night. Are you sure you are up for the march today?"

"I have to be there Claudia. Do you know how many letters we've gotten in the last few weeks since the article about our prison stay?" Claudia rolled her eyes. "And did I tell you what happened yesterday when Alice and I were leaving the office?" Claudia shook her head. Helen shared the story:

A fancy automobile with a uniformed chauffeured driver had pulled up just as Alice and I stepped outside. The window rolled down just a few inches and a silken glove hand poked out.

"Miss Paul, I presume?" a gravelly voice with a clipped accent asked.

"Yes," Alice responded.

"I'm Mrs. Vanderbilt."

"Hello, hello Mrs. Vanderbilt," Alice stammered. The window then rolled all the way down until Alice and Helen could see the woman behind the voice. She was older, wearing a wide brimmed hat made of dark blue wool and a fur stole.

"I recognized you from the papers and had to come visit you in your office myself," she spoke slowly, enunciating each word distinctively. Alice nodded her head.

"I wasn't used to seeing Alice speechless!" Helen exclaimed.

"I was quite shocked by your mistreatment—and the other women too," she said, inclining her head toward Helen. "I realized how little I've done to support my fellow woman in her right to vote." she stopped to take a breath. Then she handed Alice a thick envelope.

"I plan on stopping by the office tomorrow and supporting your cause further. Well done, Miss Paul. Well done." Before Alice could respond, Mrs. Vanderbilt rolled up her window and the car sped off.

"*The* Mrs. Vanderbilt?" Claudia asked. Helen nodded. "We are so close to the vote being passed. Now remember bring an extra sweater!"

"Mama, I'm fifteen! Stop treating me like a baby! Besides who do you think was in charge when you were gone?" she said, her hands on her hips. Helen threw her head back and laughed. "Yes my dear, you are right!"

"Goodbye, Albert! We'll be home before supper," Helen cried out cheerfully, with Claudia and Eleanor in tow. After dropping Eleanor off with Iris, they made their way to the suffragist office on 23rd Street.

"I'm so happy Papa isn't angry anymore," Claudia said.

"Absolutely! I don't even want to think what I would have done if he hadn't let me come home and live without my family," Helen agreed.

"Are you all right with not traveling? Or not working as much with the suffragists?" Claudia inquired.

"Oh Claudia. That's complicated. Truthfully, I'm not sure if physically I could handle the travel now and I still get to work with them. So, I suppose it's a compromise. It's the reality in our lives as women," Helen acquiesced. "Look we're here."

"Hello Ladies. You all have met my daughter Claudia," Helen said and Claudia waved. This wasn't her first march. Helen had started taking her to rallies over the last year.

"Let's see, you know Lucy Burns and Alice Paul," she said. "Plus Mabel Vernon, Crystal Eastman." Claudia could see their scars and limps but today the women were beaming with heads held up high. As soon as they showed up to the office, they saw a small motorbus parked outside the building, taking them to march uptown. The women quickly boarded; Helen and Claudia joining them.

"Helen, do you remember the parade in Washington after Wilson was elected back in 13?"

"Yes—good god, I thought I was going to be trampled to death," Helen chuckled. "Lucy, if you hadn't spit on that man, I wouldn't have done it right after you! I almost spit on the policeman too," Helen reminded her and Lucy Burns laughed.

"You would have spit on a policeman?" Claudia asked. Helen nodded with a smirk.

Mabel Vernon, who was sitting directly across the aisle from Claudia and Helen, started singing softly "Let Us All Speak Our Minds." A few minutes later, all the women on the bus joined her. Claudia got goose bumps looking over at her mother singing along with the women. They barely had music playing in the apartment so she didn't see her sing often. As soon as the song ended, Crystal Eastman, sitting two rows in front, started them on "Promised Land," and one song melded right into another. When there was a lull in between songs, someone would chime in to share a story of a rally where the number of women attending surprised them or talk about an incident where they were bullied, yelled at and spit on. The bus kept stopping and picking up more passengers. Claudia didn't want the ride to end.

She looked at her mother's longer skirt compared to the other women's more fashionable short dresses and her unadorned hat in contrast to the other women's tight-fitting decorated hats. Helen still hadn't regained the weight that she had lost in prison, and her clothing hung loosely on her lanky frame.

Was this woman the same one who cleaned their apartment, cooked their meals, darned their socks? This woman— her mother—now sat with her shoulders back and composed. Claudia watched her laugh alongside these women, and she could see the others look at Helen with respect and authority, asking her for details about the day between songs, and soliciting her opinion. They wanted to hear more about the aftermath of the articles in the newspaper and Helen's opinion when President Wilson would support the suffragist vote. "Any day now," she kept saying with certainty.

"She works so hard—here at work and at home," Claudia thought. While she had been to a few rallies over the years with her mother, she was just learning today how important her role was in the organization, and it made her feel sad. It wasn't right that she was the daughter sitting on this bus next to her mother, singing along with these women, jubilant about marching for the right for women to vote. Abigail should be here—she was the one who had fire in her belly. She was the one who had stood up to her parents. She was the one who had died.

"Claudia. Baby, what's wrong?" Helen said and touched her arm. She felt her mother dab a cotton handkerchief and wipe away the tears from her face she didn't realize were there.

"It's just not fair Mama."

"What? What's not fair?"

"Abigail..... Abigail should be the one marching today by your side. Not me."

"Oh Claudia! I miss her too. More than you know. I think about her every day. It took me a long time before I gave myself permission to be a part of this group—to let myself be happy again and accept that I deserved to be here. I spent many years letting guilt weigh me down like a ton of bricks. You have every right to be on this bus, every right to march alongside these women, every right to fight for our right to vote. Every right to feel proud of the valuable and important work you're doing, we're doing. Don't forget that," Helen said rubbing the side of Claudia's head, pulling her close. Claudia tried to stop crying and let her head drop on her mother's shoulder, finally letting the cloth muffle her sobs.

"Helen, are you joining the march in Connecticut next week? From Hartford to New Haven?" Lucy Burns inquired.

"Why New Haven?" Claudia asked.

"That's where Senators McLean and Brandegee live. So far, they won't vote for our amendment. The Connecticut league has asked for our support in rallying in the capital and then marching to their hometown to shame these men."

"I can't." Helen answered, touching her leg. "I'll be supporting you back at the office and in spirit!" Claudia knew she was also keeping her promise to Papa to stay in town.

"Here put this on," Helen said as they got off the bus and handed her a white banner that read "Votes for Women." Claudia put it over one shoulder like her mother. Helen moved to a bench on the sidewalk close by and sat down.

"C'mon Mama, they are getting ready to leave," Claudia said, anxious to join the group getting ready to march.

"You go on without me."

"But I can't, not without you."

"I don't think I can march today. My leg is acting up and aching something fierce. This cold isn't making it easier."

"But Mama, I don't know these women."

"Yes, you do. They'll look out for you."

They heard a few cattle calls from the crowd:

"Ladies—go home."

"Get off the street, unless you plan on working them."

"Most women don't want to vote—they'll only vote like their husbands."

"Yar wasting your time."

Alice Paul stared at the negative naysayers and said with a strong dignified voice, "Women have the right to vote. Your wife would want you to vote for us."

Helen then paused for a moment and continued steadily, "You know, when I started going to rallies and marches, all these men—and women—yelled at us that we couldn't be there. I believed them at first and was so ashamed. But then I realized that I did belong there, we belonged there. To stand up for our rights. We aren't doing anything wrong." Claudia looked around nervous, eyes widening. Helen looked her right in the eyes and said, "Don't worry about those skeptics. They'll always be there. Instead look at them," and pointed to a group of people, mostly women with a few men peppered throughout holding up signs supporting them.

"Just ignore the others. After a while, you don't hear their voices any more. Just concentrate on all the faces in the crowd that are smiling back and waving at us," Helen continued with an experienced tone. "Besides, this crowd is quite tame, I've seen much worse. Your father will be so proud of you and we'll be home in no time."

Lucy Burns came up and put her arm around Claudia's shoulders. "I'll take good care of her Helen. We'll march a few blocks and then come back to check on you." Helen nodded.

"You can do this without me. I'll be here watching for you my love," Helen said. Claudia leaned over so Helen could kiss the top of her head as if to bless her. She buried her lips in Claudia's hair and planted an abundant number of kisses.

"Go on, go on," Helen said waving her hand. Claudia put her wool hat on her head, adjusted the white ribbon around her shoulder and waist and turned around to join Lucy and the other women that had already started marching. She ran to catch up to them. She turned around to look at her mother. Helen waved and blew a kiss. Wait, was her mother crying?

Claudia started shouting the slogans she heard all around her, "Votes for Women." "Suffrage First." "Equal Rights for Women." Her cries got louder and she blended in with the other women marching. Alice Paul linked her arm through hers and Claudia beamed up at her.

EPILOGUE

1918

World War I ends.

President Woodrow Wilson ultimately states his support
for a federal woman suffrage amendment. He then
addresses the Senate about adopting woman suffrage.

1919

The Senate finally passes the Federal Woman Suffrage
Amendment, the Nineteenth Amendment, and the
ratification process in the states begins. It was originally
written by Susan B. Anthony and introduced in Congress
in 1878.

August 26, 1920

Henry Burn casts the deciding vote that makes Tennessee
the thirty-sixth, and final state, to ratify the Nineteenth
Amendment to the Constitution. American Women win
full voting rights.

ACKNOWLEDGEMENTS

There are so many people who helped me along the way and this book never would've happened without any of them.

Brooke Emery Scharfstein. You told me a writer writes and encouraged me to sign up for a writing class. With love and gratitude.

Julie Sarkissian, Jessica Noyes McEntee, Eve Legters, Allison Dickens and Westport Writers Workshop. You are amazing women who have taught me, guided me and created a writing community that I'm immeasurably grateful to and for.

Deborah Alexander, Kiki Tsakalakis, Gwen Mitrano, Madeline Monde, Michelle Didner, Margie Jacobson, Betsy McBrayer, Kris Jandora, Robin Hellman, Amanda Shapiro, Eden Abrahams, Amy Abrams, Ruthie Kalai, Deena Kalai, Mary March. My writing lights. My beta readers. My cheerleaders. We've gotten to know each other's characters like they were family members. The circle of support and gentle prodding we have created, I am forever indebted to.

Elise Gichon Strauss (aka Mom). I'm grateful to you in instilling a love of reading, being a strong female feminist role model and your love and ongoing support.

Yael Gichon. For always being the person I could turn to and sustaining a sister friendship that allowed me to write this book.

Sophie and Hannah Clemens. My daughters. This book is for you. You are amazing young women that are the future, the next generation, the hope we have that women will have equality in our society and that minorities will be recognized as equals. You inspire me daily and I learn from both of you in different ways at every turn.

Nikki Gorman. You supported my writing by first finding me a babysitter so I wouldn't miss class, to encouraging me to find time to write, to finally getting to know Helen as one of your own friends and taking on the suffragists cause as if your own. You motivate me to become a better writer, get my voice out there and push me to reach for the stars. I couldn't have done this without you and our love.

Adam Clemens. You have always been a cheerleader providing unwavering support and love. You always encouraged me to follow my passion and accepted my hare-brained new ideas with positive reaction.

ABOUT THE AUTHOR

 Widely quoted in *The New York Times* and more, Galia Gichon spent nearly ten years writing financial research for top investment banks Bear Stearns, Nomura Securities and Institutional Investor before launching Down-to-Earth Finance, a top personal financial & investment advising firm in New York.

In addition to *The Accidental Suffragist*, Gichon is the author of *My Money Matters*, a personal finance book which received notable press from the *New York Times*, TODAY Show, CNN, *Newsweek*, *Real Simple* and more. Gichon produced a popular Creative Live course, and consistently leads seminars for Barnard College where she has taught for 13 years, and other organizations worldwide.

CPSIA information can be obtained
at www.ICGtesting.com
Printed in the USA
BVHW030210020621
608621BV00005B/70

9 781948 018968